DAD

ALWAYS & FOREVER

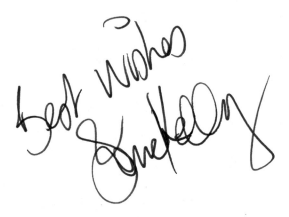

CHAPTER ONE

Lena was woken by loud voices coming from the next room. *'Not again!"* She muttered under her breath, pulling the duvet cover up over her head trying to block out the shouting and swearing coming from her parents' bedroom. In all honesty, it was more her mum's voice which she could hear more than her dads. This was the norm, and Lena was at the age where she understood the meaning behind the words and the reasoning for the fights, but this only made it worse for her!

As she lay in her bed with the duvet covering her head, she tried to block out the noise and began to imagine herself far away from this place she called home and Glasgow all together. In her dream she placed herself on a white sandy beach, just like the one in the book she was reading. Imagining how it would feel having the sun shining down on her skin and the sound of the waves she eventually drifted off to sleep...

Opening her eyes, the morning daylight shone through her bedroom curtains, she felt relief that she had dozed off to sleep. Lena yawned and stretched, wondering what she would find downstairs after all the drama from last night. Slowly, she got out of her bed, walked over to the small chair in the corner of her bedroom and dressed herself in the same clothes she had worn yesterday.

Upon opening the living room door, she knew something was not right, she felt it in her gut. **OH MY GOD!** Her mind began racing, as she looked around the room she was struggling to take in the scene before her eyes.

The whole living room had been turned upside down, there was broken glass from the picture frames which were previously on the wall. All the ornaments her mum had bought from charity shops were lying in pieces on the floor, along with the stuffing from the cushions which had been torn apart. Panic was building inside, she began wondering where her mum and dad were, then she heard a faint whimper from behind the overturned sofa. Cautiously, Lena made her way fully into the room and dreading what she was going to find, she popped her head over the edge of the sofa to find her mum, lying half naked with blood all over her face and hands.

'What the bleedin' hell happened here?' She asked, but her mum could not answer her, she turned her face towards Lena's' with tears streaming down her cheeks. 'Mum! I don't know what to do! Will I phone the Police?' Dread and fear were coursing through Lena, she felt scared and helpless.

'Help get me up from here...NO POLICE! You

hear!' Warned her mum, as she struggled to turn her body, from the twisted position she had been lying in.

'OK! OK! Let's try and get you out from behind here... Eh?' Lena used all her strength to turn the sofa around, then gently helped her mum up from the floor and round onto the sofa where she fell back moaning in pain.

'Mum, where's Dad? Was it him that did this to you?' Lena was not sure she wanted to hear her mum's reply, but she had to ask. Someone else might have been involved or was she wishful thinking, deep down she thought she already knew the answer!

CHAPTER TWO

The next few days after her mum's attack, life in the Davis household resumed as normal. Lena's younger brothers Brian and Ian were still needing to be fed and watered, as usual Lena got up every morning to make sure they were dressed and had something to eat before going to school. Once she saw them running up the street to catch the bus to school, she would then start trying to coax her mum to get up out of bed and join the land of the living. This was a daily routine, which Lena hated, as her mum was usually still drunk from the previous nights' drinking session. Lena's patience was often tested to the extremes, as she cajoled her mum to get up, washed and dressed. Since the attack though, it was harder for her mum to physically get up from her bed.

"C'mon Mum...It's time to get up. Brian and Ian are away to school, and you need to get up!" Lena felt as though she was talking to herself, as she watched her mum pull the duvet cover up over her head. "MUM! I am not moving from this room until you get up...I'm sick of this! This isn't the way it should be, and I don't know how much more I can take from this life anymore, with you feeling sorry for yourself!" Tears of frustration fell silently from her eyes down her cheeks as she stood at the side of the bed taking in the sight of her mum, Lena shook her head and wiped her face on the sleeve of her jumper. *Why me?*

Lena loved her family, but this did not stop her fantasizing about what it would be like not to have alcoholic parents and a life like this one.

Ever since she was little Lena knew there was something different about her Mummy and Daddy. There were always bottles and glasses she was not allowed to touch, but when her parents drank from them, they became funny Mummy and Daddy. Growing up she was always surrounded by her mum and dad's friends. There would be a party most nights, where the adults would be drinking and dancing, some would play games with her, life was happy. It was a different story in the morning though. Lena would get up from her bed, walk into the living room and there would always be adults and empty bottles lying on the floor for her to step over to get to the kitchen. When she entered her mum and dad's bedroom to try and wake them up, they would always shout at her and tell her to go away. Lena learned from an early age how to get the cereal and milk together to fill her achy belly. Deep down, even away back then, Lena knew her life was dictated by alcohol, she just did not understand the full impact, but she liked her funny Mummy and Daddy better than the angry, sad ones!

When Brian and Ian came along, life did not get any easier.

The arguments between her parents became a daily occurrence because having the three kids was getting in the way of their drinking. It was hard trying to look as though they were coping with one kid and their need for the drink. When Brian came along it got a bit harder, but now with three kids it was nigh impossible. It was just after Brian was born, when her mum had brought him home from the hospital that a lady started visiting them and Lena sensed her mum and dad did not like this lady. It was on the days when the lady was due to visit, she noticed that her parents did not drink anything in the morning, like they usually did. The house would get the once over with the hoover and she would be warned to behave and not say a word. Once the lady was out the door normal life would resume and she would watch her mum and dad race to the fridge and cupboard for the funny drink. They would drink and before long they would be chatty and laughing again, whilst Lena and her brothers were left to their own devices once more.

Lena was aware that her homelife was different from other peoples.

This became clearer when she started school and began visiting her new friends at their houses. She noticed how clean their houses were and attentive their parents were to their needs. Nothing like the chaos which she called 'home' was like. The Davis household was cluttered, messy and in need of a good clean not to mention the never-ending noise caused by her parents arguing! Whereas, her friend's mums took pride in their home's appearance, Lena's mum, Fran, was more likely to be found with a gin bottle in her hand than a cloth or hoover. Lena loved being invited to a friend's house for dinner because she was provided with a homemade meal, something she never got back at her house. The differences between her world at home and those of her school friends was enormous, but she still loved her parents...faults and all!

There were five years between herself and Brian and seven with Ian. Lena had taken on the role of protector and made sure their basic needs were met from an early age. When Brian was a baby, she looked after him, treating him like one of her dolls. When her mum was too drunk to pick him up when he was crying, she was the one to wrap him in her arms and cuddle him until he settled. The same with Ian, she made sure they finished the food put down to them by her mum and she would be the one to make sure they had cuddles and felt loved. Feeling the responsibility from such a young age was hard, and in many ways had stopped her from having a childhood, but she loved her brothers with all her heart and would do whatever it took to make sure they were safe and stayed together, as there was always the lady who would pop in to see them and chat with her mum.

Leaving her mum lying, Lena turned and stormed out of the bedroom towards her own room, banging the door as she left. "If you want to be like this then you can lie there! You're pathetic!" Lena felt her blood boiling with rage at the injustice of it all! Most days she just got on with life, the fact it was the only way she had ever known was neither here nor there! As she pottered about her bedroom making her bed and giving it a tidy, she was away in a world of her own daydreaming.

Suddenly, there was a loud bang coming from her mums' bedroom. **_What the bloody hell was that now?_** She ran to her mum's room as fast as she could. Upon entering, she found her Mum lying on the floor on her side, "Mum, what happened? Have you hurt yourself?" She asked worriedly, as she carefully tried to help her mum into a sitting position on the floor.

"Ouch! Watch Lena! My back is killing me! I tried to get out of my bed and my legs gave way on me...It's so feckin sore...I'm scared to move!" Lena had witnessed her mum in lots of precarious situations, but she had never seen her like this, vulnerable and asking for help! "Mum, I'll need to go get an ambulance, because I don't know how to help you move, I don't want to hurt you! I'll be back in a minute," Lena ran from the room and called 999. Within an hour, the ambulance had been and carted Fran off to the hospital for an assessment to find out what was going on with her.

CHAPTER THREE

Upon hearing the post dropping behind the front door, Lena fastened her dressing gown tight around her waist before making her way to see what he had brought today. With her dad disappearing money was tighter than normal, every morning there was another bill urgently needing paid. Lena knew it would all come to a head eventually, but for the moment she would throw them in the drawer, where there was a growing bundle of them. Amongst this morning's letters one stood out from the rest...Opening it she felt her blood turn cold. ***Jeezo...This is all she needs now***! When her mum saw the letter, she knew it would make everything worse. Quickly she placed the letter in her pocket unsure what to do with it...***I'll deal with you later!*** "Returning to her bedroom, she got dressed and began her usual routine of getting the boys up and ready for school.

It had been three weeks since her mum had fallen out of her bed. After numerous tests and scans they discovered her spine was damaged and the nerve endings were causing her extreme pain. It was suggested it could have been due to some kind of trauma. Both Fran and Lena had looked at each other when the Doctor had stated this, both aware it was probably the result of the attack in their living room when Lena had found her mum behind the settee, that was traumatic after all!

Lena had tried to locate her dad unsuccessfully. Since the night of the attack, months previously, he had not been heard or seen of. This was not unusual behaviour for their dad, he often went missing for weeks or months. He would go with whoever had enough drink to keep him going and slept around with other women, much to her mum's dismay and broken heart. Usually though Lena or Brian would hear in the streets of his whereabouts. This time they had not heard anything and had no idea where or who he was hiding with! ***Time would tell***... Lena had told herself and Brian. He'll need to crawl out of the woodwork eventually, he would come home when he needed them! The fact that they needed him, and he was not here was second nature to them all. They would need to pull together just like they usually did!

Brian...Will you take this up to Mum? If she asks, tell her it was Mary next door that made it..." Lena placed a knife and fork onto the tray next to the shepherd's pie, that their neighbour had kindly handed in. Brian sauntered into the kitchen and lifted the tray moaning, "When's Mum going to get up from bed? This is a pain!"

"Not as much as the pain she's in at the moment, the Doctors said she has to rest, then fingers crossed, she'll be able to get up. Now take it up and smile eh!"

"Did she eat it Brian?" Lena asked, walking into the living room holding her own dinner plate. "Well, she sat up and took it off me...She asked when she was due more painkillers though! I think she's using them instead of the drink now! Do you not think so?" Lena shook her head in disbelief. The Doctors were well aware of her mum's need for alcohol, and whilst she had been in the hospital, had been giving her tablets to help her cope with the alcohol withdrawal symptoms. They seemed to help her when she was in, but now that she was home, she was finding it difficult not resorting back to her old habits. Brian could have a point though. Another thing for her to worry about. Lena just shoved it to the back of her mind for the time being. Feeling in her trouser pocket, she ensured the letter from the Social Worker was still safely there. She could not let her mum know about it yet...Another problem to worry about!

"Well... How was your dinner?" She did not wait for her mum to reply, she lifted the half-eaten plate of food up from the bedside table. "You'll need to start eating more Mum, you need to build up your strength!" Fran lay looking up at the ceiling, "Have you got my tablets there? They don't seem to be touching this pain Lena, I think I need stronger ones." Lena reached into her trouser pocket to get the tablets. The sound of paper rustling made her mum turn to look in the direction of the noise.

 "What was that? What you got in your pocket?" Lena took a deep breath and produced the letter from the Social Worker. "This came this morning, but I didn't want to worry you more Mum." Fran grabbed the letter, "Why, what is there to worry about?" Lena watched as her mum took in the words written on the paper, then saw how her demeanour changed.

"That'll be feckin China...If they think for a minute, they are gonna take my kids away from me, then they can feckin think again! I'm telling you Lena, you ain't going nowhere!" Fran was shrieking at the top of her voice, as she threw the letter onto the floor. "But Mum It says they're coming to visit us and make an assessment. It's been a while since they've been out, it'll be ok, won't it?" Fran stopped shrieking, "Don't open the bleeding door Lena...I mean it! Last thing we need is that lot sticking their beaks in, we don't need their help!"

Lena looked wide eyed in disbelief at her mum, "Mum we do need help...Maybe if we find some ourselves then the Social will leave us alone," Lena was feeling overwhelmed ever since her mum had come home from hospital, "You must know someone that could help us out, just until you get back on your feet."

Fran looked at her daughter standing there before her. At fifteen she should be out with her friends, carefree and having fun. Instead, she was left to look after her brothers and now her mother. Fran knew that she placed too much responsibility on Lena's young shoulders, but she had no other option. It was either this way or the Social would take them and put them into care.

"What about Uncle Jack?" Lena had heard her parents talk about Jack, her dad's brother throughout the years, but she had little memory of seeing him herself. Right now, he was the only person she could think of to reach out to since her dad was nowhere to be found, he was family after all!

Fran felt a chill run through her. "Uncle Jack? Why would he want to help us Lena? "The last time she could remember seeing her brother-in-law was when he was running away from her! "Perhaps he would help us at least until we find Dad." Fran could hear how scared Lena was, and if the truth be known she was terrified of losing her family herself. *Maybe I should get in touch with him, see if he's up to sorting this mess out which he helped create*, she thought to herself.

CHAPTER FOUR

Jack Davis sat nursing a half n half at the end of the bar, in 'The Nag's Head', just off Renfield Street in the town centre. This was his usual drinking den. He liked the fact all the regulars knew his name and more importantly, knew WHO he was! Jack loved the notoriety and the feeling of power he felt was the one thing he lived for on a daily basis.

He had started off small...

Years previously, as he sat supping his drink in the pubs of Glasgow, Jack would watch the other men come in and spend most of their weekly earnings, before heading home, full of the drink and ready for a fighting match with their missus. Week after week he watched, and it was always the same individuals and always the same pattern of events. He had no one at home waiting on him or his money, so he came up with the idea that he could help these men out whilst helping himself too!

Gradually, over the space of a few weeks, he had himself a nice little earner going. Casually, he would approach these men and open a conversation with them. As the night went by and the drink flowed their tongues would slacken and they would soon be spilling all their marital problems out to Jack. Pub after pub, it was the same rigmarole, until eventually Jack would offer them a way out of their wives' bad books! The men were usually so drunk and desperate for some cash for their pockets that they would agree to anything. So, Jack would offer them a solution, week after week, with the interest growing daily!

Soon... the name Jack Davis instilled fear into the hearts of many a drinker in Glasgow's city centre pubs.

Jack became well known for his money lending and feared for the repercussions of failing to meet payments on time! Through time, Jack began having problems getting his loans paid back on time, so he enlisted the help of some guys who had no problem in extracting his money in any manner they saw fit. This resulted in a few men being beaten black and blue, whilst others ended up with a hospital stay, yet no one would mention the reason behind their beatings or the name...

Nowadays, Jack lives an extremely comfortable lifestyle on the outskirts of the city with his long-term partner Sylvie. They had met one night in 'Victoria's Nightclub' on Sauchiehall Street. Sylvie was tall, blonde with curves all in the right places for Jack. Watching her on the dancefloor in her tight, low cut red dress, he could feel his excitement build within himself, as she moved seductively looking directly at him, he knew he had met his match!

 Since that fateful night they had moved quickly. Sylvie was well aware of Jack's reputation and had no qualms about being in a relationship with a man like him! After all, up until now he had never been violent with her and she found him to be extremely generous, both in the bedroom and with his money, there was nothing not to like! Weeks and months passed into years.

Six years on...Sylvie still enjoyed spending Jack's money. Anything she wanted she bought, it was with a deep sense of envy that the one thing she really wanted could not be bought for any amount of cash...her and Jack's own baby!

Sylvie and Jack were good at putting smiles on their faces, but the smiles never reached their eyes. Outside looking in, it looked like they had it all! They were both good looking, took care of themselves, with regular visits to the gym, they were also well-known big spenders, especially in the designer stores of the Merchant City area of Glasgow. They had social lives some would envy but if the truth be known, they preferred being at home. Sylvie had an eye for interior design and had turned their detached property into a very luxurious home, which she loved spending time in, albeit she felt lonely at times and knew the house was missing something. Both felt a deep sorrow, that they had been unsuccessful in making a family, it was the one thing Jack wished more than anything he could give to Sylvie. He knew she would be a fantastic mum... She had all the qualities, and she was a good homemaker, all the things his own mother had lacked. There was no way in hell he could ever break her heart, by giving her the news that he had fathered a baby with someone else...

Jack knew if Sylvie ever found out he was already a father, it would destroy her and their relationship. He had never officially been informed that he had become a father, it was all hearsay. As far as he was concerned the baby had a father living with her and her mum, so why mess up his life over some rumours! Although deep down, he knew it was a very strong possibility, there was no way he could allow this information to get back to Sylvie, she knew too much about his business and finances as well...He would do everything in his power to make sure she never heard any of the rumours, he had to protect her and more importantly himself.

CHAPTER FIVE

"MUUUUM...Will you please tell Ian to stop annoying me..."

Fran shut her eyes tight, willing with all her strength for the two boys to stop their carrying on and give her peace. "The two of you had better well start behaving! Do you hear me?" She knew she would be better off talking to the wall, as she got no reply from the two boys in the next room. Every day was a struggle for her. Ever since she had damaged her back, Fran could not begin to explain the amount of pain she was suffering, both physically and mentally.

Sure, the painkillers helped at first, but nowadays, they only took the edge of the searing pain throughout her body. That is why she had started taking them with alcohol. Together they both numbed her; body and mind. "Lena will be back in ten minutes from the chippy, if you don't stop you won't get anything to eat...It'll be straight to your beds!"

Laid up on the settee, Fran dreaded to think of the state the boys had made of their bedroom. She was frustrated, at the fact she could not physically be involved more in keeping them busy and out of mischief. Life had not been easy for her or the kids before being in pain, nowadays it was tough as hell! Fran hated the way in which she had to depend on other people, Lena, she was not willing to let outsiders see just exactly how bad her life and that of the family had gotten.

Between Lena and herself they had convinced the Social Worker that they were coping with the needs of the kids and themselves. However, they were still under their watchful eyes as they visited every fortnight. Fran was under no illusion, they were visiting far too frequently for her to have any peace of mind, and this was causing her immense stress, resulting in more sleepless hours, and taking more painkillers/alcohol, it was a never-ending cycle she just could not break from.

On the last visit, the Social Worker had asked repeatedly about the whereabouts of Tony, "Don't you think I'd like to know as well?" Was her reply, but she could sense that the Social Workers patience was wearing thin with all her excuses. Fran knew if she did not come up with an answer on Tony's whereabouts soon or had an extra pair of adult hands for support, the kids could find themselves in care. The only person who could maybe have knowledge of Tony's whereabouts, was the last person in the world she wanted to ask for any kind of help from, but she was beginning to feel trapped with no other option!

Lena let the door bang behind her as she returned from the chip shop with tonight's dinner. She could hear her brothers shouting and screaming from along the street. "Brian! Ian! SHUT UP!! I could hear you both from the other end of the street, close the windows and get your backsides down here for your dinner!" Fran felt relief flow from her at her daughter's return. Lena could surely handle her brothers, much better than she could, and she would be handing over her new prescription of painkillers, she had hopefully picked up from the chemist! Brian and Ian burst into the living room carrying their bags of chips, still in the wrappers, smelling of vinegar, they sat crossed legs in front of the tv.

"Are you two happy now?" Both boys nodded their heads up and down in agreement. "Good! At least that is one thing you can agree on..." Chuckled Fran, as she lay on the settee, with a hot water bottle at her back, watching her boys munching their way through their chips, she marvelled at their happiness in the simplest of things and wished she could have played a part in creating this memory for them. The overwhelming sense of failure hit her once more, the frustrations at her lack of mobility, due to her back and the chronic pain it caused her and her family, powered through her.

"Lena... Did you get the chemist doll?" The pain was flaring up again and with her feelings of frustration on top, Fran was desperate to get her hands on the only things that could ease her pain and numb her mind! "Yeah Mum...Two minutes and I'll bring your tablets in with a glass of water." Lying waiting, the only thing Fran could do was fantasise about her life before pain, and how easy her life could have been if she had only made the right choices back in the days! Opening her eyes as she heard Lena's footsteps coming through from the kitchen, Fran decided there and then, that she would need to set her pride and resentment aside for the sake of her kids. "Lena doll, once the boys are settled, I need you to do something for me..."

Lena looked quizzically at her, "Mum, I am always doing something for you, it's about time you started pushing yourself and doing things! You need to start trying to move about and take care of yourself now!" Fran could see Lena was stressed and at the end of her tether, she knew she relied too much on Lena, that she should be out doing things with her friends, not looking after her and her brothers. Leaning towards her daughter, she whispered, "I know you're fed up with everything here Lena, but if you can just do this one thing, it'll help both of us...I promise you!" When Lena looked at her, Fran winked at her, "I promise!"

CHAPTER SIX

Outside the weather was wet and horrible. It had rained nonstop for the full day and Sylvie was not happy, as she had made plans for an evening in the garden, to entertain some friends of theirs.

"Sylvie Darling...Why not just change the date to next Saturday, instead of getting your knickers in a twist over the bloody weather! No-one will mind, in fact it'll probably suit folk more, than getting all dressed up and having to come over in this pissing rain..." Jack was not up for seeing anyone tonight, never mind having to act the host. The turn in the weather suited him and how he was feeling, he just had to convince Sylvie!

"Jack, people will have already planned their babysitters and transport, I can't just tell them we aren't hosting a night now!" This was exactly the reply he was expecting to hear from her, "Sylvie...I'm not asking you now, I'm telling you! Cancel tonight! Blame the weather, whatever, I don't really care, just make sure nobody turns up here expecting a bloody party tonight, ALRIGHT!" Sylvie stood open mouthed in shock, watching, as Jack got up from his executive chair, slamming his office door closed in her face.When he was like this, she knew not to answer him back, as the last time had resulted in a full-blown shouting match, which had led to her hiding behind her Gucci sunglasses until the swelling and bruising had gone! Rather than go through the trauma of that again, Sylvie closed her mouth and made her way upstairs to the bedroom, to call her friends, and make excuses for the late cancellation notice, all the while muttering under her breath ***Feckin arsehole***!

After downing his second whisky in one go, Jack laid his head back on the headrest, took a deep breath and closed his eyes. Underneath his Ralph Lauren shirt, his heart was racing, with a rage he was finding hard to control. He didn't want to inflict anymore hurt or pain on Sylvie, like he had the last time they had argued. He loved her; he really did! Deep down he knew he had totally lost it for reasons which had nothing to do with her, if only she had kept her mouth shut, he would not have had to slap her! ***Feckin woman doesn't know when to stop***! He was repeating this to himself, even though he knew the **REAL** reasoning was all down to him and his actions!

Earlier in the month, he had been made aware of some rumours that his brother, Tony Davis, had vanished off the face of the earth. No-one had seen or heard from him, this worried Jack, because Tony owed him money, but more importantly, he had delved into Jack's past and was trying to hold a family secret over him. The problem facing Jack was who had Tony told about this, because he couldn't hold his water, he knew he would have told someone...BUT...His main issue right now, was that the word on the street, was that Tony had met his maker! If this was true, then the Old Bill would be looking for suspects for his murder, no doubt, Jack's name would be top of the list!

Just as he was about to pour himself another drink, the sound of the doorbell stopped him dead in his tracks. "Sylvie! Thought you were telling folk not to come!" He screamed down the hallway. The clicking of Sylvie's high heels on the staircase was all he could hear. Thinking that she was ignoring him and going out somewhere, he walked from his office, along the hallway, and stood at the bottom of the staircase, watching her, as she glided by him, without uttering a reply to open the front door.

Upon opening the door, there stood a young girl Sylvie did not recognise. "Can I help you doll?" She asked, narrowing her eyes for a better look. The girl was in her mid-teens and not dressed for the weather. It was still raining heavily, it was cold, yet the girl standing in front of her had only a thin bomber jacket with no hood, old trainers and was drenched to the bone! "I've been sent with this note for Mr Davis..." Unsure whether to invite her in out of the rain, Sylvie decided the safest option was to keep her standing at the door, as she called over her shoulder, "JACK! It's someone for you!"

Placing the whiskey decanter onto the mirrored sideboard, Jack lifted his half full tumbler and walked towards Sylvie, to see who was visiting him at home. As he approached the front door, he did not recognise the young girl, however, he could tell she was of no threat, so he invited her inside out of the rain.

"So...you've come all this way in this weather Hen, it must be important! Although, I've no idea why!" He said, studying the girl's features, there was something familiar about her, but he could not for the life of him put his finger on it!

"My name is Lena...Lena Davis, my Mum's sent me with this note!"

At that moment, Jack knew why the girl looked familiar. The only sound was the shattering of glass as his tumbler slipped from his fingers...

CHAPTER SEVEN

Lena realised they were in deep trouble when her mum told her about her plan to get in touch with her Uncle Jack! It had been years since they had last seen him, in fact she must have only been about 2 or 3 years old the last time they had contact with him. With her dad out of the picture now, he was the only other person she knew of who might be able to help them, so she agreed to whatever her mum had in mind!

Stepping out of the door, into the cold wet night, Lena was dreading her journey to the posh side of town, but there was a little piece of hope within her, as she felt in her jacket pocket for the note her mum had given her. ***Please, Please, Please be okay about this***! Played over and over in her mind, as she quickly made her way to the bus stop. Once on the bus, the adrenaline, which had helped to keep her moving through the wind and rain outside, began to subside and her mind went into overdrive. ***What if he doesn't recognise me? What if he turns me away***? Round and around, the questions spun in her mind, the higher her anxiety levels were rising, as the bus made its way through town.

Eventually, the bus was approaching her stop, Lena took several deep breaths to try and calm her racing mind. When the bus stopped at her destination, Lena jumped off into the cold and rainy night again! Taking the note from her pocket, she checked the address once more, to make sure she was heading in the right direction, then proceeded to what she prayed would be the answer she was looking for!

Approaching the house Lena's heart was racing, although it was wet and cold, she could not feel it anymore. ***Well, here goes***! She thought to herself, as she pressed the doorbell...

Lena saw the look of horror on the woman's face the moment she opened the door to her, she decided there and then to play it cool and calmly asked for Mr Davis. The woman looked high maintenance, with her dyed hair, full face of perfect make-up and fancy clothes, Lena felt intimidated by her beauty, but quickly reminded herself of the reason for her untimely visit.

Standing in the pouring rain, the woman instructed her to wait, as she shimmied away from the door. Lena could see the outline of her uncle walking towards her with a glass in his hand. He opened the door fully and welcomed her in out of the rain, for which she was so thankful, because she was soaked through. As they both stood in the hallway staring at each other, time seemed to stand still, *He looks a lot like me*! Lena recognised the similarities straight away, his eyes and mouth were the same shape as hers, as was the colour of his hair. When she had answered his questions, as to why she was here at his home, Lena was as shocked as him at his reaction!

The sound of the glass shattering, into a million small pieces, brought the woman running back out into the hallway. "WHAT THE HELL IS GOING ON?" She shouted, running towards where Lena and Jack stood in shock surrounded by glass. "Sylvie! It's fine! Go!" Jack was trying to take this moment in and what it meant for him, the last thing he wanted was Sylvie playing drama queen!

Turning, he looked to his left side, where Sylvie was, he could tell she was ready to go off on one of her tirades, "GO! NOW! SYLVIE!!" He shouted, straight into her face, as she stood mouth wide open, "FUCK OFF! NOW!" The spit flew from his mouth, as he shouted, the atmosphere was tense, Lena could see the anger in his face which terrified her. Uncertainty flooded her, she was just about to turn and run, when she put her hand into her jacket pocket. Feeling the note from her mum, she reminded herself of the reason she was here. Taking a deep breath to try and slow her racing heart, Lena produced the paper from her pocket, looking Jack straight in the eye. She nervously offered it to him, "My Mum sent me here with this note for you!" Slowly, Jack raised his hand and accepted the note from her, "Listen kid, why don't you come through into the kitchen, try and get dried off whilst I read this?"

Lena wasn't sure what to do, she feared this man standing in front of her, particularly after the way he had spoken to the woman Sylvie. She also felt the pressure of her family's needs upon her shoulders, her wet, heavy shoulders, so she decided to give him the benefit of the doubt, at least she would get dried off before having to face that journey again!

CHAPTER EIGHT

Dear Jack,

It's been a long time since we saw each other and a lot has changed, the main thing being your brother has disappeared again, only this time I have a feeling he won't be coming back anytime soon! The kids are good, Lena is a wee godsend, I'd be lost without her! The thing is...I've not been keeping well, not just the drink this time, my back is damaged, I struggle with everything. I don't like admitting this to anyone Jack, so I'm hoping you will understand just how bad things really are for my family and why I'm asking you to help. Lena will fill you in!

Fran

Jack sat on the couch as he read the note, then reread it once more, trying to read between the lines, for any other meaning behind it. Across the lounge, Lena sat on the stool, next to the open fire, trying to dry herself off. Every time he looked up from the letter, he caught her staring at him, then quickly looking back into the flickering flames of the fire.

"OK kid, so what's been going on with your Mum then?" Lena turned towards him. "Firstly, can you stop calling me kid please? I'm approaching sixteen, so I'm not exactly a kid, my name's Lena!" She realised this might upset him or put him off helping them, but his use of the word was grating her, she struggled with responsibilities no kid should have to put up with!

Jack smirked, as he thought to himself, **she has her mother's attitude alright**! Fran was always a fiery bit of stuff, with plenty of attitude to give amongst other things. Part of the allure, which had attracted him to her in the first place, but that was in the distant past until now. "Sorry! Forgive me Lena...Tell me what has been happening at home."

After Lena had finished explaining what home life was like, and the amount of responsibility she carried on a daily basis, he knew he could not turn his back on their cry for help. He would always carry a soft spot in his heart for Fran, they had shared memories, some fun but most troublesome, due to her love of drink. Fran could do things for him and make him feel things he had never experienced with any other woman, but once the drink took hold of her, she would turn into someone unrecognisable, the reason he walked away from her the last time. Thinking back, Jack was hesitant to go near Fran once more, he had to be sure he felt strong enough, within himself, to deal with her again. Looking at Lena, sitting in front of him, no matter how much she protested, she was still a kid, a kid with an uncanny resemblance to him, he owed it to her to go back!

"What do you say I give you a run home, see how your Mum's doing...Eh?" Jack got to his feet, put the note into his trouser pocket, the last thing he needed was for Sylvie to get wind of that, it would send her into meltdown. Better he saw Fran for himself and exactly what kind of help she needed before telling Sylvie anything. She was the jealous type, he had witnessed this first hand, when she had hit the ceiling and there was nothing to be jealous about, he still wasn't sure how he would feel when he met Fran again, Sylvie could be reaching new heights!

CHAPTER NINE

Looking out from the living room window, Fran watched, as cars zoomed up and down the road outside, there amongst them a big flashy car, which was slowing down and parking outside her gate. *OH MY GOD!* Fran could feel her heart racing, she felt as though it was going to explode inside her chest, sweat began forming on her top lip and down the sides of her brow. The more she tried to control her breathing the worse it was getting! Fran had always experienced slight anxiety, but since the accident and having to watch her alcohol intake due to the pain medication she was taking, it was getting worse, the slightest thing could start it off! Right at this moment, as she watched Jack and Lena get out of the car and walk to her gate, her heart rate increased tenfold, she told herself to get a grip and slow her breathing down. *Breathe*! *In and out*! Fran moved slowly from the window to the settee, repeating her breathing mantra in her head, inhaling, and exhaling deeply. Just as she heard the front door open, she felt her anxiety level lessen slightly, she knew she had to put on her best front for this moment. Coming face to face, with the man, who was responsible for so much carnage in her life!

The moment he walked into the living room, Fran took one glance at Jack, standing there in front of her, as handsome as ever, still carrying the same degree of arrogance and all her feelings of anxiety simmered down.

"Hello stranger! It's been a long time Fran"

He was taken aback, at Frans appearance, as she sat in front of him, on a settee which had seen better days. He had listened, as Lena had described how her life was and what her mum had gone through, yet the frail, unkempt woman he saw in front of him still took him by surprise. In his mind, Fran had always been a good looking woman, one who looked after herself the best she could given her love of the drink.

Thinking back to the first time he had met her, he was impressed by her beauty, more so her 'go get them' attitude to life, just like himself! Fran always knew what she wanted and how she would get it, come hell or high waters, she would get whatever she had set her heart on! Jack admired this quality in her because he recognised the same one within himself! Their first encounter had been full of spontaneity and passion, yet it was the same thing, which tore them apart further down the line as well.

"Hello Jack! I wasn't expecting to see you again like this!" Fran looked from Jack to Lena, trying to work out in her mind what the hell she was meant to do now. Seeing him in his expensive clothes, looking sharp, she felt embarrassed, not only at her tired looking home, but at her own worn out appearance. She dared not try to move from the settee, as she did not want him to witness her painful struggles in moving herself. Throughout the years, when she had played this scene out in her mind, she was more like her old self, before the accident had robbed her of her nice looks and confidence. It was, as she looked at Jack, she realised that the results of the accident had taken more than her full mobility, it had taken her identity!

"I'll put the kettle on...Tea or coffee?" Lena sensed her mum's insecurity in the meeting, trying to bring some level of normality to a far from normal situation, making a cuppa always helped ease the tension in the soaps on the tv, it was worth a try she thought.

"Coffee for me Lena, two sugars and milk please," came Jack's response, as he wandered over to the window.

"I'll have my usual Hen. Are you checking up on your car? I'm sure no-one will steal it, if that's what's bothering you?" Jack chuckled to himself at Fran's questioning, she might not look much like the Fran he knew, but that attitude was all he had to hear to know she was in there somewhere, all he had to do was pull her out of herself!

Fran's lower back was aching, she managed to grab the cushion next to her on the settee, slowly, she placed it behind her back, whilst watching Jack eye up his surroundings. Inside, she was cringing with embarrassment at the untidiness and dowdiness of her house, aware that Jack would be living in luxury, with the best furnishings his money could buy, probably with a dolly bird to match. Deep down inside, she was still the same Fran he had chased, until she had given into his seductions, although she looked and felt as worn out and dowdy as her home, at that moment.

"I found a packet of biscuits in the cupboard, it's your lucky night!" Lena joked, making her way back through to the living room carrying a tray with coffees and biscuits upon it.

"Uch I'm okay doll, no biscuits for me, trying to keep myself in shape" Jack laughed, whilst patting his stomach. "All the more for us then mum before Brian or Ian catch sight of them." Lena passed her mum's coffee mug over to her and offered the plate with the sweet treats on it. Jack lifted the remaining mug and sat back more comfortably in the armchair opposite Fran.

"So where are the boys then? Hiding in their rooms?" Enquired Jack, before taking a gulp of his coffee. "They are with their friends just down the road, they'll not be home for another hour or two yet. Their friend's Mum has been really good at letting them play in the house," replied Fran, relieved that the boys were not at home right now!

CHAPTER TEN

The hours seemed to fly by, as they chatted about their lives, whilst Jack discovered more in depth about the situation, he had found himself right in the middle of. Whether he wanted to or not, he could not walk out of this house and never return, he knew he was this family's last hope of staying together.

"Right, so when is the Social Worker due back Fran? The quicker we can get this place looking a bit more organised, the better and that includes you too!" Jack knew deep down he couldn't just walk away from Fran and her kids, after all he owed her!

"A week on Monday, she's coming back to check on the kids and there's no way she's taking them away from me! I'd rather kill myself, than watch her place my kids in care Jack!"

"She won't be taking them anywhere Fran, because you and I are going to ensure this place looks the business and the kids...Don't worry about it! First things first though...How much are you still drinking, and how many of those prescription tablets are you throwing down your throat a day?"
Taken aback at his directness, Fran could feel anger and resentment building within herself, "Who are you talking to? Think you can come in here and accuse me of all sorts..."

"Listen, I'm not here to argue with you Fran, you

asked for my help remember. The least you can be is feckin honest with me and yourself for once! I've eyes in my head, I can see what you're doing to yourself with the drink and meds, so are you going to own it?" Jack knew he had to remove the kid gloves, when it came to getting her to face up to her addiction problems. At this moment, he wasn't feeling great about the way things were going, but he recognised that if he was to have any chance of helping her and the kids out, then he had to be tough!

 "Lena darling, why don't you go get the boys from your neighbour, give your mum and me a wee bit of time to talk eh?" Lena wasn't sure whether to leave them alone or not, she could see the way in which her mum was frowning, but she was also well aware that things couldn't get any worse than they were right now, so decided to grab her wet jacket and leave them both to sort it out!

Fran stared straight at him, he could see the rage in her, yet he did not flinch a muscle, he just stared straight back at her, until she started shaking her head, "I've been trying, like really trying hard to help myself get better. It's ok for you to come here, see me like this and you're probably thinking the same old pathetic Fran! Well, I'm nothing like the old Fran from way back... That is part of the feckin problem, you have no idea how I feel every day and the pain I'm in! "
Jack stayed where he was, although he wanted to go over and give her a hug, he could see the

anguish, it was written all over her face, but he had hit a nerve in her and as much as he wanted to comfort her, he knew he had to try to get her to open up, in order to confront, exactly what she was doing to herself and the kids!

Softening his tone of voice, "Fran, I'm here to help you, like you asked, so why don't you tell me what life's like for you then...like REALLY like! If I'm going to be able to do anything here you need to be truthful, I need to know exactly what we're up against, and I mean WE! You need to be up for doing as much as you can to change this situation for the better, that means getting rid of the junk you're putting into yourself or at least using the meds as they're meant for!"

Listening to his words, Fran knew he was right, and burst out crying.

Jack got up from where he sat, he crossed the living room, to sit next to her, placing his arm around her. He tried to comfort her, as she cried, until she could cry no more tears.

"I know I'm a mess Jack! I know what I need to do. I just don't know how or where to bloody start, I'm scared! Ever since that night, when I hurt my back, our lives have gotten worse and I feel terrible, 'cause if I hadn't been so drunk in the first place, it might not have happened and now look at us! I feel even more useless than before, because at least before, I could walk and move about easier to look after the kids, but now they have to look after themselves and me, I'm a bloody burden on them, specially Lena, she shouldn't have to look after me and her brothers the way she does, it's not fair on her and it's all my fault Jack!"

"The main thing is getting you better mentally, the rest will fall into place from there. Kids are resilient Fran, they love you and just want to see you trying, we all do, and you can do it...if you put your mind to it!"

"You don't get it! Most days I don't even want to be here! When I wake up in the morning, it takes me all my effort to put a smile on my face and try to get out of my bed. Then if I can get out of bed that day, due to the amount of pain all over, the most I can do is lie on this settee. I'm in feckin agony right now because I've been sitting like this...That's what you don't get, everything causes me pain...Everything! I take a drink to block out the pain and top up with my meds to block out this mess of a life! So how are you going to fix me?

When Lena arrived back home with the boys in tow, she sensed an air of calm in the house. Upon entering the hallway, she could hear her mum and Jack talking, not like they had been earlier, but more in agreement with one another, she took this as a positive sign and her feeling of dread lifted as she walked into the living room. "We're home!" She announced, as Brian and Ian followed her into the room.

"Aye, so we see...And who have you brought with

you!" Jack asked, jokingly. The two boys stood at either side of her, eyeing up the stranger in their house. Pointing at each of the boys, Lena introduced them, before telling them she would make them tea and toast if they got ready for bed. The boys smiled at their big sister before racing along the hallway to get their pyjamas on.

"You're a great big sister to them Lena! Things are going to work out better for all of you. Me and your mum have been chatting and came up with some ideas to try to make life easier for everyone...Haven't we Fran?" Stated Jack, as he gave Fran a gentle nudge.

CHAPTER ELEVEN

Two weeks passed since Jack had answered Fran's cry for help and surprisingly, she had kept to her side of the agreement. The day after his visit, she had called the Doctors surgery and made an appointment to see her GP, hoping to take back some control over her drinking and abuse of pain medications. The Doctor was keen to help her and made her a drug reduction plan, hoping to reduce the meds and incorporate other more alternative ways of managing her pain levels, she referred Fran to a Pain Consultant and explained how this would help her long term, in getting some kind of normality back into her life.

Jack had to admit to himself how impressed he was, with Fran's new attitude and the actions she had taken so far. He had been shocked, when she had opened up about how low she really felt deep inside. When they had discussed ways in moving forward to help her and the kids, he actually hadn't held out much hope, but she was surprising everyone around her with her positive new approach. He was praying it would last, yet he wouldn't get his hopes up that much, he reminded himself it was Fran after all, he had other problems to contend with closer to home!

Sylvie had become even more of a nightmare since he had gone with Lena to see Fran. When he had returned home that night, in the early hours of the morning, he assumed she would be asleep, he could not have been more wrong. She was sitting waiting for him, ready to pounce the moment he entered. That night and every day since she had accused him of sleeping with Fran, to the point where they no longer shared a bed. The atmosphere in the house was icy and no amount of heat was going to defrost Sylvie, she was adamant that he was cheating on her, and he knew her too well to think things between them would get any better soon... If at all!

Sitting at his desk, within his home office, Jack was pondering how his life had changed recently. If he was honest with himself, he always had feelings for Fran, even though he had not seen her in years, she was always in the back of his mind, somewhere. It was impossible not to think of her now and again throughout the years, it was only natural, after all of the times that they had shared together.

Taking a gulp of whiskey, from his favourite glass, he questioned his feelings about her today. Recognising he had alternative motives in helping her and the kids, especially Lena. There was something about that girl, her attitude and more so her resemblance to himself!

The sound of the telephone ringing

saved him questioning his motives any

further...

"Boss...we've got a problem!"

"It better be worth you disturbing me at home for Daz! Believe me, I'm in no mood for bullshit right now!"

"Boss, I think you need to come down here and

see this for yourself...It's big! The container's been done, there's gear all over the place...it's like a feckin snow globe in here!" Panic stricken, Daz had no idea what had happened, or more so who had the nerve to turn the place upside down!

"I'll be there in 10..." Jack leapt out of his chair, rage building up inside him, his mind went into overdrive, trying to work out who the hell was out to get him now! One thing was certain, when he found them, they would be sorry they were ever born!

As far as he was concerned, there was only himself and Daz that knew about the container and its contents. He had made the decision not to involve any of his other men at this point. They would be told on a need to know basis, right now, they did not need to know! He had decided to get into the cocaine scene, due to the amount of money he could make. It would be easy for him to distribute, using his contacts he already has within the money lending circle. He knew for certain; the punters would be chomping at the bit to get their hands on it, easy money...So he thought!

Racing through the city centre streets, Jack's mind was in turmoil, trying to work out who would have known about his side deal with the cocaine. It had taken him months, making solid contacts in Liverpool. In order to access the dealers, he wanted, he had spent hours wining and dining the big bosses to try and gain their trust, this had cost him time and money. At the time, this didn't worry him, as his thoughts were solely on the benefits, which he would gain!

It was pitch black, when he arrived on the south side of the town, at the lock up site. Suddenly, he was blinded by beams of bright light, as Daz flashed his headlights, to help direct him towards the container. "Boss...You are not going to believe your eyes; it's all bloody wasted! There's no way we're going to recover from this!" Daz was babbling, which was getting on his nerves.

When Daz opened the door Jack could not believe his eyes, the place was covered in cocaine; it looked like the blocks had been slashed open, then swung around the space where they now stood. "Whoever the fuck did this better have left the country!" The rage had risen within him, he was shaking, struggling to control his anger. All around him it was covered in dustings of the white powder, everywhere he looked, he saw wasted money. He could not comprehend how this had happened. He was struggling to come to terms with the amount of money he had lost in this vendetta against him.

"I canny believe this has happened! No-one and I mean NO-ONE knew about this but us...I pray for your sake Daz; you haven't been blabbing your mouth off where you shouldn't have been!"

"Boss...I swear on my kids' lives, I've not uttered a word of this to anyone. I know how much this means for you and the money involved, I know

you! I value my life too much to mess this up for
you or myself!" The sweat was glistening on Daz's
brow and top lip, deep down Jack believed him,
he had known Daz too long, and they had shared
too many dealings together, he would never turn
on him, of this he was certain! At this precise
moment, as he surveyed the room, Jack was at a
loss as to who had just signed their death
warrant!

There was not one person on his radar he thought
daft or brave enough to take him on in this
way...He would kill them himself!

CHAPTER TWELVE

Things were improving slowly for Fran in her
recovery, she was regularly frustrated at the
Doctor, as she felt he was not taking her as
seriously as she thought he should. At the first
appointment she had felt positive that she could
beat the drink and drugs, however, as the time

moved on Fran was struggling with the reductions made by the Doctor, the withdrawal symptoms were still there, albeit not as severe, as going cold turkey. There were days at the start when she curled up in her bed, wishing she had never allowed Jack to talk her into this, as the sweats and shivering worked their way through her body. Eventually, her system settled enough, allowing her to think clearer, which meant she could look at other ways to manage her chronic pain.

Nowadays, instead of lying in her bed, waiting on Lena bringing her meds and breakfast through, Fran got herself out of bed, albeit slowly. She had discovered a way of rolling onto her side, before easing up into a sitting position, from there she could stand with crutches for support.

Every morning, Lena prayed that her mum would still be positive and up for the fight, which faced her that day. She was impressed by the way in which her mum had been trying up to now, but she worried that she would relapse back to her old ways. This was something that none of them wanted, as life was becoming bearable for them all.

"Lena...I'm up! "

"Thank you, Lord!" She whispered, as she got out of her bed and made her way next door to her mum's bedroom. "Look at you! You're getting good at this now, ain't you Mum?" Pride was in Lena's voice, she felt better being able to assist her mum in getting dressed for the day ahead. It was much easier helping her and giving her encouragement, than bringing her pills and resenting her for giving up on life, which was how she had been feeling before Jack had stepped in to help.

"Where are the boys? Are they up yet for school?" Fran asked, as Lena helped her slip her top over her head. "They're both still in bed, why don't you give them a knock, once we've got you dressed, you know they like it when they see you before school now," It was true, life was resembling something of a happier, more functioning family now that Fran was off the drink and working to control her pain. There was still a long way to go before the Social Workers stopped visiting all together, but they were only calling in once a month at present, which pleased them all, especially Fran, she could see her hard work was paying off.

Once the boys had left for school, Fran began her stretching exercises the physiotherapist had given her the week before. Sitting on the chair in the living room, it involved slow arm and leg movements, she had lost a lot of muscle in her limbs, due to lying in bed for so long. Lena stood at the kitchen door watching, admiring her mum's determination as she struggled with the moves. It was clear to see the pain on her mum's face as she attempted lifting her legs and arms, "Come on Mum, you have got this! You can do it!" Fran looked at her daughter and wanted to cry, mostly from the pain she was in, but more so at the way in which she was encouraging her, she felt she didn't deserve it. "It's not happening Lena! I should be able to do this for Christ sake..."

Rushing over, Lena wrapped her arms around her mum's shoulders and kissed her on the forehead, "Mum it's going to take time, the physio guy told you that. The most important thing is that you are trying your best, you are definitely doing that, so you can hold your head up high 'cause we are all proud of you and you are improving every day!" The tears fell from Fran's face, but for once they were happy tears, "As long as you kids think I'm getting better, that's all that matters to me. When the Doctor explained about the spine being like a caterpillar, with the legs being nerve endings, due to it being out of alignment and that's the reason why I'm in so much pain, it helped me get my head around it a bit more. I'm going to beat this the best I can...I promise you Lena!" Wiping tears of frustration from Fran's cheeks, Lena reassured her once more, "I know you will Mum, we are all in this...We're a team!"

"Who's a team? We talking football here girls?

Both Fran and Lena turned towards the voice, surprised, to find Tony peeking around the living room door!

At first, she thought her mum was going to miraculously spring up from her seat and attack him. The look of utter hatred on her mum's face, told her that her dad was lucky she couldn't get to him. at that moment in time.

"**YOU!** You had better be bloody well joking with me right this minute Tony Davis! Where the hell have you sprung from?" Fran was taken aback at seeing him again, there was no way he was getting away with it. Not this time!

Lena stood with her mouth agape, in total disbelief, at the sight of her dad, standing in the middle of their living room, as though the past several months had not happened. He looked the same as always, perhaps a little rounder, so wherever he had been staying he was being fed. Lena's mind was going into overdrive, with questions she had for him; however, given her mum's reaction, there could be bloodshed in the house today.

"Mum, calm down! He's not worth you getting yourself all upset over!"

"Calm down! You're bloody lucky I canny get moving fast, because I'd kill him with my bare hands!" Turning to face Tony straight in the eye, "You can take yourself right back out that door! Think you can disappear all this time and we are going to welcome you back with open arms, think again!" Fran's heart was racing, she was struggling to remain in control of herself.

Tony stood laughing at Fran's reaction, "You're forgetting whose names on the door love! I'm not going anywhere soon so get used to it!"

Lena shook her head and walked into the kitchen; she had heard all this so many times in her young life. Right now, her main concern was how his return would affect her mum's road to recovery. She had been doing so well, they all had, now they had support from Uncle Jack, this could mess everything up for them all. Her mum and dad together usually did!

CHAPTER THIRTEEN

"Are you having a laugh Daz?"

Jack was still reeling from his find within the containers the week before. Every day that had passed was spent trying to find some intel, as to who had the nerve to step on his plans for expansion. Jack had sent out all his men to ask around town with the exception of one...Daz. He was not one hundred percent certain Daz was being honest with him, regarding not blabbing the coke deal to someone. He thought he knew

Daz well enough, they had been through a lot of dirty dealings together, enough to guarantee silence, if pressure was ever upon them, but Jack was questioning everyone at the moment, he felt he could not trust anyone and that included his right-hand man!

However, the news Daz had just shared with him on the phone sent Jack into a total rage. The moment Daz had finished relaying the news that Tony had been seen sauntering down Bath Street in the Town, without a care in the world, Jack threw the telephone at the wall across his office!

Sylvie came running into the office when she heard the loud bang and scream from behind the door.

"What the hell Jack! What's going on?" She asked, watching Jack pacing the office floor, face beetroot red with rage, she knew something bad had kicked off.

"What's going on? That feckin brother of mine...THAT'S what's going on!"

This was making no sense to Sylvie, "What are you on about Jack, he's dead is he not?"

"Apparently NOT! But I am telling you, he will be when I see him!" The look in Jack's eyes, when he replied, scared her enough that she quickly turned on her heels and promptly left the office.

The timing of Tony's reappearance was not being ignored by Jack, he had basically fallen off the face of the earth for months, not one reported sighting of him, and now he's strolling about town as if it were the most natural thing in the world! Nothing about this was normal, Jack was beginning to think his brother was part of a much bigger plan to get to him!

Lifting his jacket from the back of his chair Jack called out to let Sylvie know he was going out before she could answer she heard the banging of the front door as he left. Shaking her head, she watched his car race from the driveway, *no surprise where he's racing to*, she thought!

Fran was still in shock from the reappearance of the man she thought was a goner, one way or the other. The minute Tony showed up, she knew trouble would not be far behind him and how right she was! Sitting across from her, he looked towards Lena, "Lena hen, are you going to make your auld Dad a cuppa?" He was making himself at home too fast for her liking, there was something going on, she sensed it! He was acting way too sure of himself for someone who had vanished, presumed dead, to just turn up out of the blue again. Lena nodded, before heading into the kitchen to put the kettle on, she was speechless!

"So...What's been happening since I last saw you all?"

Fran stared at him full of hate and disgust, how could he disappear without a trace leaving her the way he had and the kids. Showing up now full of himself, she knew he was up to something and that meant trouble for her.

"Well, where would you like me to start? The way you left me for dead after beating me up good and proper, leaving me like this now! EH?? Is that what you want to talk about OR the way you left your kids in the lurch again!! EH?
Which one would you like to start with Tony? You tell me!" She was seething at the amount of arrogance he was showing.

Smirking, he replied, "Well...it is nice to see you too Fran, still your charming self I see. Good to know some things never change, all the problems in the world are still down to me! I never left you for dead! And as for the kids...Lena looks fine, I'm assuming the boys will be too, so that just leaves you and let's be honest you cause all your own problems through the drinking! Don't you?"

She was aware he was taunting her, deep down she wished she could remain silent, but her pride would not allow for that.

"You think it was the drink, you're partly right. I was drunk the last time I set eyes on you, but it wasn't the drink that beat me black and blue, then threw me over the bloody settee...That was YOU! You utter piece of shit! You have no idea what the kids and I have suffered whilst you've been shacked up with some floosy! Now you think you can just waltz back in here and everything will be fine... Well, it's not happening this time, Tony! We've been through too much to let you in again to destroy what we've got now!"

"We've been through? What we've got now? Who's the WE Fran? Sounds like you've found yourself a new man, eh? Even in the state you're in, you're still after the men, eh? Well, it doesn't surprise me, you could never survive without one!" He sat forward on the seat when Lena appeared with his cup of tea, "Oh...No new man here Tony, we've been getting through ourselves, just me and the kids.... with a little help from a friend!" Fran could not stop herself now, she saw the crease of his forehead, as he tried to work out the meaning behind her words. "Friend! Aye, very good Fran! That what you're calling them nowadays...Friends?" Laughing, he put the cup of tea to his mouth, "Well actually he's more family... You see it's your brother Jack!"

Across from her Tony coughed and sputtered as he nearly choked on his tea!

CHAPTER FOURTEEN

Lena stood in the kitchen out of sight, but within hearing distance, of every word that was being spoken in the next room. There had been days when all she wanted was for her dad to return and help them, seeing him now she could not help herself for wishing he hadn't turned up, like the proverbial bad penny. The boys would be happy to see him, she was certain of that, they missed having him around, for all he was worth! She on the other hand realised there was more to his return than met the eye. Past experience has shown her a more sheepish man, when he finally found his way home in the past, looking for forgiveness from her mum, but today his demeanour was too self-assured and there was definitely no sign of him seeking forgiveness!

In the midst of her mum and dad arguing, suddenly it stopped.
Lena heard the living room door opening...

"So, it is true? You've decided to crawl out of the woodwork and come back to your wife and kids!" Lena heard her uncle Jack's voice boom across the living room. ***Oh my God! This is NOT good...***

Slowly, she made her way into the living room, to find Uncle Jack standing next to where her mum sat, both staring across at her dad waiting for him to respond.

"Are you just going to sit there? C'mon we're all dying to know where you've been the past few months Tony, the least you can do is tell us!" Lena could hear the menace in her uncle's voice, she was praying this would not escalate into a fight, right here in her home.

"I would say it's none of your business, but it appears you've slipped your big dirty feet right under my family's table! You've always been jealous of what I had, even her!" He replied, pointing at Fran.

Jack took two steps towards where Tony sat, "Jealous! Of YOU!" He screamed, "Believe me, you have feck all to be jealous of...Not one feckin iota! You have NOTHING! Never have had either! You might have lived here, when the fancy took you, but you have NEVER been a family man Tony! You had it all for the taking, a missus and three great kids, but you didn't even have the sense to acknowledge how lucky you were. You always put yourself before your family, never here when they needed you! So, aye I have stepped up, where you've fallen BROTHER!"

The atmosphere in the room was thick with menace, Lena walked over to where Fran was sitting ashen faced, and slowly sat down next to her. Tony's face reddened with anger, he looked from Jack to Fran then towards Lena herself. "MY FAMILY! MY KIDS! Are we all sure that's true?" Staring straight at Fran, he continued, "What's up darling...Cat got your tongue? Not like you to be quiet...Eh Fran? I'm not surprised finding you here playing the big hero the minute my back's turned BRUV! Not the first time either, is it now?"

Tony got to his feet and was now almost face to face with Jack. Fran suddenly burst out crying, "That's enough! Both of you, do you hear me!" Getting to her feet with the help of her crutches, she made her way towards where Tony was sitting, placing her body between both men." Jack had to step in to help us, if he hadn't the kids were going into care, because I wasn't fit to look after them due to my health, so stop this, Tony!" But her plea had fallen on deaf ears, "OHHHH STOP! I'll stop when I decide... NOT YOU! The truth is too much for you to handle, poor wee Fran!" Glancing at her side where Lena sat, Fran replied, "It's not me I'm thinking about!"

Jack tried to intervene," Tony! You've said more than enough now, put a zip on it!" He spoke calmly, not wanting the situation to explode right now in front of Lena, who was sitting looking puzzled.

From the moment he had set eyes on Lena, Jack noticed the resemblance to himself. When Fran had told him she was expecting a baby once their affair had stopped, they had both decided it was in everyone's best interest not to tell anyone. After all, she had begun dating Tony, the baby could be either one of theirs. Tony was making it quite clear now that he knew the real identity of Lena's Father. It was only a matter of time before Lena became aware of the truth, he did not want her finding out this way!

CHAPTER FIFTEEN

Sitting, Lena watched as the faces around her all changed expression after her dad had spoken. Mum looked worried along with Uncle Jack, yet her dad stood glaring at her mum with a smirk across his face.

"Will you get me some painkillers doll?" Fran asked, forcing her to get up and leave the living room. Once in the kitchen Lena could hear them muttering to one another, they were talking so quietly she could barely make a word out. Inside, her gut was screaming, warning her that trouble was on its way! Feeling uneasy she carried the glass of water and medication into her mum. "Do you want to lie down for a rest Mum, you've done quite a bit today?" It felt like forever, yet it was only hours previously when it was just the pair of them practising Fran's physiotherapy quite happily. Now the atmosphere in the room was fraught with tension, with the length of time Fran had been sitting added to her increase of pain.

Fran washed the painkillers down with a large gulp of water, " I think I will hen, I'm done in!" Usually, Fran would have put on a brave face, pretended she was okay, before admitting her pain to anyone, but she was way past the point of caring what either of the men thought of her anymore, she did not have the energy to care!

Lena helped her mum by slowly helping her stand up onto her feet before guiding her into her bedroom to lie upon her bed. "Are you comfy? Do you need me to get you anything else Mum?" Fran shook her head, reaching out she grabbed Lena's hand, "I'll be fine here as long as I have you! I love you, Lena! You know that don't you?" Lena was taken back by her mum's words and seeing tears in her eyes.

" Mum...I love you as well, you rest, and we can talk later."
Closing the bedroom door Lena made her way back towards the living room in the hope of getting some answers to the questions buzzing around in her mind.

Jack remained standing, looking out of the window whilst her dad was sitting down on the settee. Both men did not acknowledge her presence until she spoke, "Right, I may be young but I'm not daft! There's something going unsaid here and I want one of you to tell me..." Looking from her uncle Jack to her dad for a reply which did not come. "I'm waiting!" It was getting dark outside, Jack turned from looking out of the window, "Lena I think you had better wait until your Mum's feeling better before pursuing this conversation, it's best she's in the room when it happens."

 Moving over to the settee Jack sat down next to Tony. Lena noticed for the first time how alike the brothers actually looked, the same dark hair and facial features, the only difference being the amount of care Jack took in his appearance whilst her dad never took any!

Lena's thought process was broken by the return of the two boys bursting through the living room door. Both boys stopped dead in their tracks, shocked...

"Dad! Where have you been?"

It was Brian who asked the one question Tony had yet to answer to anyone. Ian rushed over to sit beside his dad. Lena watched as Tony placed his arm around Ian and pulled him in for a cuddle much to Ian's delight, he had really missed having his dad around the place, he was the only one!

"Yeah, Dad where have you been? Answer your boy then!" Jack had his own suspicions as to where Tony had been spending his time, he was keen for his brother to reply...
"Uch...you know me Son, here n there! Had to help a pal of mine out of a wee bit of bother, but hey...I'm back and I am not leaving you again!"
"Aye you mean anytime soon? We all know you'll disappear again sooner or later so don't be making promises to the lad you can't keep!" Lena was enraged at the sheer arrogance of her dad, thinking her mum would just accept that he was back, and he could stay in the house with them. There was no way, after everything they had

suffered recently, that he would be welcomed back into the fold with open arms. She hoped!

It appeared to her that her mum held all the answers and at the moment it was a waiting game!

CHAPTER SIXTEEN

Business for Jack was going from bad to worse and fast!

Word had spread about the cocaine being busted, there were rumours that Jack had gotten involved with big time drug dealers from down south and they were not happy with him setting up his own area to distribute. Jack knew this was nonsense and just gossip. Every day there was another drama to deal with. People that owed him large amounts of money were playing hard to find, making it impossible for him to recuperate his finances, he was trying to juggle too many balls at once causing him an enormous amount of stress. The last thing he needed right now was for Tony to turn up and start causing him more grief, especially with Sylvie. He knew that it was only a matter of time before the truth came out regarding Lena and the trouble it would cause between them.

"Daz...what's happening with collections? We need to get money fast!"

On the other end of the phone his right-hand man was out pounding the streets trying to get any information on the whereabouts of people that owed Jack big time. It was not going well as most of them had gone to ground, trying to hide from the beatings which had their names on them!

"Gov, I've tried all known places, it seems they've all changed their drinking holes, I've even knocked at a few houses and guess what? Yeah, that's right, no one's home either! They've all fecked off good and proper!"

Pacing up and down in his office Jack could hear the exasperation in Daz's voice. He knew he would kill the first one that did show face. Daz was not to be messed with, the fact he was out searching would not be doing his patience any good, so God help them when he eventually did get them.

Jack knew this from past experiences, if they tried to hide, it was a matter of time before Daz made them disappear for good!

"Right! Stay on it, someone has got to appear sooner or later! I'll be in touch if I hear anything!" Slamming the phone down Jack's stress levels were ready to explode, the pressure was on, and he needed all his problems to disappear fast.

There was no mistake that there were people out to get him, but he could not shake the feeling that they were closer to home!

"Jack honey, I'm just popping into town to meet some of the girls, do a bit of shopping and grab some lunch, won't be too late back." Sylvie called, before he heard the slamming of the front door. *Thank Feck*! The last thing he needed was her hanging about asking questions. At this moment in time his business problems were larger than his personal ones, yet he knew that could change once Sylvie got word of them.

He had not heard from Fran or Lena in two days, guessing that no news was good news, and that meant Tony was not around anymore!

How wrong he was...

The morning after the night before Fran awoke early and slowly got herself dressed then made her way into the living room only to find that Tony had taken up residence on the settee. The pills which Lena had given her had made sleepy and she had slept through the whole night, unusual for her as she usually tossed and turned. Seeing Tony on the settee brought it all back to her, the shock and unanswered questions which were going to test her relationship with her daughter. Until she had discussed things with Lena and ensured that their relationship would survive, she knew she had to try and play Tony, just until she felt more confident with the situation. The hatred she felt for this man lying in front of her was insurmountable. The more she thought back to all the pain and suffering he had caused, she could quite easily kill him herself, but she knew his time would come eventually!

Fran stood at the living room door watching him where he lay, wondering what the hell he was up to and more importantly with who!

Driving into Glasgow in her new BMW convertible Sylvie looked a million dollars. She had spent extra time getting ready today ensuring that there wasn't one hair out of place and that her makeup was flawless. Whilst doing her makeup she chose red lipstick to match her skirt, her favourite perfume completed her look and helped to make her feel powerful which she needed today of all days! It had taken her months of planning, but eventually everything was falling into place.

CHAPTER SEVENTEEN

Fran approached the sleeping Tony on the settee, "Wakey! Wakey!" Nudging him until he opened his eyes. "Who told you to sleep there? I want you out! So, get ready and GO!" All the hardships the kids and herself had been put through because of him had built up inside to resentment and disgust. Tony remained lying where he was, "You canny tell me to get out, this is my home and my kids, well at least two of them are! Thought I'd never find out, didn't you? Well, it's a good job there's folk in this family that do tell the truth!"

Fran had no idea who he was talking about, as far as she was concerned it was only Jack and herself that knew about Lena, there were no other family members to speak of. Watching him as he got up from the settee he made his way into the toilet, she knew she was going to have to be careful how she played this with him, the last thing she wanted was to lose Lena when she discovered the truth. Quickly, she decided that she would be the one to tell Lena everything she had to know by herself, his input would not benefit anyone and certainly not Lena!

When Tony returned to the settee Fran told him, "I want you out today! "
"I'm not going anywhere and there's nothing you or anyone else can do about it" He was smirking, as he lay back looking her up and down. "Aye well, we'll see about that once I call the Police, I'm sure they'd be interested in finding out where you've been all this time, after all you've been reported as missing!"

"Missing...You really reported me missing?" He sat upright.

"Well, they got involved because the hospital contacted them. I don't think you're getting the seriousness of what you did to me this time! One call to them and they will be here to lift you for grievous bodily harm!" Fran was trying to remain in control of her voice without shouting, "NOW, get yourself up off my settee and OUT of my house before I make that call...I'm serious Tony, GO NOW!" Pointing at the door, she was surprised as he put his shoes on and moved towards it, "I'll be in touch this is not over by a long shot, and you can tell your boyfriend the same! You're lucky I've got somewhere I have got to be today, but I'll be back!" Slamming the living room door as he left.

Relief washed over Fran, thankful that he had heard her, but in her mind, there was still an element of fear, she knew he would come back again and that only meant more trouble for her.

Startled by the loud bang Lena shot up and out of her bed thinking it was her mum falling. "Mum! Mum! Are you ok?" She was calling, running across to her mum's bedroom. Seeing the bed empty, she made her way towards the living room when Fran opened the door, "I'm here love and I'm fine. What do you say we make a cuppa and sit down eh?" Hearing the nerves in her mum's voice she understood what she was about to hear was going to be tough. "We don't need tea Mum; I want you to be honest with me. I know there's something going on with Jack..."

Gently, Fran placed her arm through Lena's and guided her towards the settee where they both sat next to one another.

"I don't know where to start Lena...but I'll try to explain it as best I can...
I met your dad Tony after I had met Jack. I had no idea they were related, let alone brothers. Jack and I met when I was doing some bar work, before the drinking took hold of me. We had a brief thing, but he was a player with all the

women, mainly because he flashed his cash about and his looks. When it finished with him, I never saw him again for months, by this time I've met your dad...Tony. We were going together, like really proper, he wasn't messing about with other women. I was with him a few months when I discovered I was expecting you. I realised once I got checked at the hospital it couldn't be his, that it was Jack's baby! I had no idea what to do... so I did nothing!"

Lena had remained quiet throughout, listening intently, "So...You never knew they were brothers? How could you not know?"
"They were never close. When I met Tony, he said he was an only child and that his parents were dead. It was only when I bumped into Jack near the end of my pregnancy that I found out they were brothers!"

Lena sat in disbelief, as a million questions went around in her mind. ***Why were they estranged? Did she have grandparents? How long had Tony known about her? Why did Jack not want her?*** The questions were whirling around and around, she was beginning to feel a sore head come upon her. Suddenly, she got up onto her feet, turning to face her mum, "Mum I need to take this all in, it's a lot! I just want to be on my own just now..."
Fran could see tears starting to form in her daughter's eyes as she watched her leave the living room.

Unsure of what she should do next Fran could feel the overwhelming urge for a drink. Sitting, the urges were becoming stronger, trying to fight against them she pondered over her past, the two men that caused her so much pain yet had given her three great kids, were still causing her pain. Reminiscing through the years it hit her, in this present moment, she was mentally stronger and in a better place within herself, she would not allow them to cause her or her kids anymore harm!

CHAPTER EIGHTEEN

Once she was dressed Lena decided she needed to get out of the house to try and clear her head. "Mum I'm popping out, won't be long!" She called, making her way towards the front door. Outside the sun was shining and there was a cool breeze. She took a big deep breath, placed one foot in front of the other, and continued walking until eventually stopping at the park gates. Entering the park, she noticed it was not busy, this pleased her, the last thing she wanted was to meet anyone she knew. Finding an empty bench, she sat down staring out at the pond. She began watching the swans floating gracefully along without a care in the world, ***oh how I wish I were one of them right now!***

Thoughts were racing through her mind. As hard as she tried, she could not help feeling bad for Tony and herself. In a way she felt they had both been cheated, herself more than him! When she thought of their relationship, she knew he would not have cared anymore, had he known the truth or not, he was not capable of giving her more than he already had. Yet for herself, she questioned the impact Jack being present as her father would have had. If he had been there, she may not have had all those years of worrying and trying to hold her family together. Jack might have been a better role model and lessened her struggles in daily life! *I might have had a childhood!*

Growing up she had always been there for all of her family, she was the one they relied upon, she loved her brothers with all of her heart. Life had not been easy, but she felt loved and had a sense of belonging. Even with her mum and dad's love of the drink she managed to get by, but now she began thinking maybe if Jack had stepped up, her life would have been a lot easier!

Mulling things over in her head she had lost all track of time spent sitting on the bench, it was only when she heard children laughing and excited screams to get to the playpark area, she became aware of how long she had spent sitting thinking. With her mind still confused, she got up off the bench and began the walk back home. She had the feeling that she would need to wait this out a bit longer, before any clear answers were given to her, especially Jacks!

When Lena arrived home, she was not sure how she would find her mum, she was expecting her to be wallowing in self-pity, maybe even on the booze so she was totally surprised when she entered the living room to find her mum with a duster in hand and in an upbeat mood. "Good you're back, did you have a nice walk?" Fran wanted her to know she was not mad at her for leaving the house abruptly earlier, she understood, and it was important that Lena knew this, they had to stick together in order to get through this mess. "Yeah, it was quiet," she answered. "Are you trying to hurt yourself?" She asked, pointing at the duster in her mum's hand, "Uch, it's only a wee bit of dusting love nothing too strenuous. Just thought I'd make a start...I am not going to let this bring us down Lena, we've been doing ok, you, me and the boys. We will get through this if we stick together ...Our family!"

Agreeing with her mum, she turned and left the room, knowing deep inside this would test them all in ways they had yet to find out!

The Davis household was relatively quiet in the days after the bombshell had been dropped. Fran and Lena decided the boys did not need to know anything at the moment. Lena had told her mum to wait until she had it clearer in her mind before telling the boys about her real dad. The one thing she was certain about was that they were still her brothers, and nothing would change between them. However, every time she thought about Jack being her real Dad she felt butterflies in her stomach, mostly nerves but also a tiny bit of anticipation for what the future would hold for them both.

There had been no sign of Jack or Tony, which was a good thing in Fran's mind. It was allowing them to come to an understanding together, just her and Lena, before they reared their ugly heads again, she wanted them to be on a stronger foundation. Something she was sure was happening, slowly but surely. After all the struggles the kids and herself had been through recently, she was certain there was a bond there which could not be broken, time would tell...

Keeping up with her newfound positivity was beginning to drain Fran. She was also aware that now was the time when she could not drop this mindset, it would have a devastating impact on her family, she could not stop! So, every day she continued to take her medications properly and practice her physio moves. It was becoming easier to manage her pain, due to the plan which the doctors had put into place for her, and her sheer determination to keep her family together.

Every day remained a struggle!

CHAPTER NINETEEN

She's too feckin happy these days...

Jack sat at the kitchen table watching Sylvie as he ate his breakfast. Looking good as always, she went to great lengths to stay slim and youthful looking, with all the latest trends in clothes and makeup. Usually, she would be asking him or moaning to him for something or other, yet the past couple of mornings, he had noticed she was singing along to the radio, happily cleaning down the worktops etc. This behaviour was so unusual for her it was making him nervous.

"Sylv...What have you got planned for today?" Turning to face him she answered, "Nothing much...You?"
Now he knew she was lying to him, she always had something on the go. If it wasn't getting her hair done, it was going out for lunch with her friends." So, you're going to be in all day today then?" He enquired, "I'll probably need to pop out for some milk, I noticed we are running low, but nothing else on..." His gut was telling him this was a lie! Something was amiss here with her, he decided he would find out today exactly what was making her so happy.

Hours passed by quickly, Jack sat in his office trying to figure out what had gone wrong with his cocaine deal. He had contacted all of his allies, asked them to put some feelers out to see if anyone had any information, yet no one knew anything about it. As far he was concerned this was beginning to feel increasingly likely that it was an inside job. His thought process was broken by Sylvie announcing she was heading out for some milk... Waiting 5 minutes, he left his office, got into his car in the driveway and began following her. ***Right, let's see what you're really up to!***

Keeping his distance, he watched as she drove right past the shop, up onto the main road then straight ahead onto the motorway.

Where the hell is she going?

Intrigued, he followed a few cars behind hers, just in case she became aware of him. Up ahead was a cut off, which he knew led to a bit of waste land, he had used it in the past, his blood was pounding, his heart rate increased, in his mind he had it worked out. He was going to find her and Daz, he was certain of it!

Slowing down, he wanted to give them enough time to get together, then he would surprise them! Slowly, he made the turning onto the waste land, just in time to see Sylvie get out of her car and make her way towards an old storage container. Jack pulled up in his car, his heart racing, he got out and made his way over to the container. He could hear voices within as he got closer, but he could not identify them, he was not sure how many were in it. Taking a deep breath, to try and calm himself down, he suddenly threw open the door and could not believe his eyes!

"WHAT THE FUCK!" He called out, at the sight of Sylvie standing in the middle of the container, standing across from her was...**Tony**!

Shocked, Sylvie and Tony both turned their heads, looking sheepish and scared, this was their worst nightmare, and it was about to come true!

"Jack...I can explain!" Pleaded Sylvie, recognising her need to get in first with a good excuse for this predicament Jack had found her in. "DON'T YOU JACK ME! YOU LYING PIECE OF SHITE! I KNEW YOU WERE UP TO SOMETHING!"

 Aware he was screaming, Jack stopped for a moment, stood shaking his head. Inside, he was trying to process what he was seeing. He was finding it hard to put Sylvie and Tony together in any kind of way, surely, she wasn't having it off with him?

Struggling to make any sense of the situation, he marched over to where Tony stood, pulled his right arm back and swung it, hitting Tony straight in the face and he began beating him over and over again. Tony fell back, landing on the dirty sawdust floor, he knew better than to try and fight back, Jack held more strength than him! With his knuckles covered in his brother's blood Jack eventually stopped punching Tony, straightened himself up, turned towards Sylvie who had remained silent throughout the beating, stating, "I will see you at home! Don't even think about not coming…I will be waiting!"

Aware the fear would get to her and that she would return home. He exited the container without looking back, as he made his way to tell Fran.

CHAPTER TWENTY

Standing, looking down at the blood-soaked Tony, Sylvie couldn't catch her breath, she was in shock! Never in her wildest dreams did she think Jack would have found out about her meetings with Tony, let alone follow her!

What the hell am I going to do now!

If she went home right now, he would still be enraged, but maybe she would be able to diffuse the situation in some way or other. It never occurred to her Jack was growing suspicious about her movements. As far as she was concerned, he was only worried about his business and that bloody Fran and her kids, especially the Lena one.

"Help me up! Don't just bloody stand there!"

Tony offered up his hand, hoping she would help him up to his feet. Sylvie glared down at him in disgust, "You seriously think I'm getting your blood on me you've got another thing coming!" She answered, turning to walk away from where he lay. "Sylvie, wait! Don't leave me lying like this, I can hardly move...Please!" He pleaded. "If I help you up you've got to promise me you won't say a word to Jack about what we've been up to! RIGHT!" Sylvie started walking back to where he lay, "You promise me?" She asked, "Yeah, yeah I promise!" He agreed, she gave him her hand and pulled him upwards onto his feet. "You know he's gonna kill us both anyway, don't you?" Tony gasped, as he tried to stop the blood from running down his face and neck.

"State the obvious, why don't you! You're right, he would kill us both, but only if he finds out the truth! That ain't gonna happen! Is it Tony?" Looking straight into his eyes. Tony wasn't sure who he was more scared of ...Jack or the person in front of him!

He knew how manipulative and dangerous she was!

Once she had helped him to stand, she could see the extent of his beating. It had taken Jack only minutes to inflict this amount of damage to his brother. If she goes home now, he could do her some real damage or worse...kill her! With these thoughts swirling around in her mind, she made the decision, she would take her time heading back home. Hopefully, by then he would be a bit calmer, and she would be more confident in answering his questions, to which she knew for certain there would be lots of!

Pulling up outside Fran's house, Jack had no idea how he had managed the drive over without hitting another car or worse a person. Inside, his mind was racing with all sorts of scenarios as to why Sylvie would be in contact with Tony. He needed to tell Fran; she was the only other person involved. Hopefully, she would come up with a better reason for their rendezvous than he had running around in his head at the moment.

"Oh, hello stranger, haven't seen you in days. Have you been hiding from us?" Fran asked him when he marched through her living room door. When she saw the look on his face, she quickly knew he was in no mood for joking around.

"You're not going to believe what I am about to tell you Fran! Are any of the kids around?" She could sense this was not good news, whatever it was!
"They're all out, won't be back for another hour or two, Lena's taken the boys to the park with their friends. You are worrying me here Jack! What the hell's going on?"

Jack remained standing; he was pacing the floor in front of where she sat...
"I'm finding this hard to comprehend Fran, I don't know where to start!"

"At the beginning is usually a good place to start! Take a breath and sit down, you'll wear my carpet out with all that pacing back and forward, whatever it is it canny be that bad!" She was trying to calm him down, yet she felt her own chest begin to tighten with anxiety.

"I can't sit down! I need to try and understand what I've just witnessed…"
"Right, well tell me then!"

"It's Sylvie!" Immediately Fran's shoulders relaxed a bit, she had no concern for the woman, so whatever this was it would not affect her.

"She's been acting weird for weeks now that I've had time to think back. Out more often, saying she's going to hairdresser appointments and all that jazz, but she's not coming back at her usual times and her hair doesn't look any different. The last few mornings she's been practically dancing around the feckin kitchen, definitely not her usual! Today I decided to follow her, find out exactly what or who has given her the spring in her step…This is the part I don't get Fran…**It's Tony!**"

"**Tony…? My Tony?** What the hell would he want with her? Is she the woman he has been with all this time he's been away? How would she even know him?" Question after question ran off her tongue in total disbelief at what she was hearing, her chest was feeling tight again.

"I don't get it either! I followed her to a bit of waste land on the south side, where there was a storage container. I couldn't believe my eyes when I walked in and saw them both there standing together!" Shock written all over his face, he continued, "The moment it registered I went berserk Fran..."

"Did you batter him? Is he still in one piece Jack? Did you touch her?" She knew he had a bad temper on him and what he was capable of, she had heard the rumours on the streets of Glasgow, and she believed them!

"He's still alive, the red mist just came over me when I saw their reaction, but I never laid a hand on her! There is plenty of time to deal with that lying piece of shit!" As he spoke his face reddened with rage, the veins on the side of his neck became prominent, she wouldn't want to be Sylvie once she got home, that's if she was brave enough to go home.

Slowly Fran got up from the couch, "Let's put the kettle on, see if we can think of any logical reason, they would be together, eh? Stop bloody pacing... sit down!"

Minutes later, they were both sitting with cuppas in hand, staring into space.

"There is no way she would be sleeping with HIM! I mean look at me and look at him there's no comparison! Half the time he doesn't even have a wash, no disrespect to you Fran, but I really struggle to see why any decent woman would want him lying next to her...Nah it's defo not an affair!"

Fran shook her head, "I don't think it's that either, from what I've heard about your Sylvie, she would not touch him with a barge pole, never mind let him into her knickers! How the hell do they even know one another? Could this be the reason he's been awol for so long?"

"I don't know Fran, I mean where has she been keeping him, if she is the reason he was away so long? Nothing about this makes any sense...But one thing is certain...I WILL find out and when I do, they'll both be sorry!

CHAPTER TWENTY-ONE

Tony sat in the pub nursing a pint and himself. He had tried his best using the wash hand basin in the gent's toilets to wash the blood from his face and clothes. From the amount of curious looks he was getting from folk sitting around him, he guessed he had not done a good job. They were the least of his problems right now!

As he sat drinking, his mind was in overdrive. Thinking back to a few months previously, when his world had been shattered, all down to a drunken slip of the tongue! He questioned his actions from that fateful night, beating Fran and now this mess with Sylvie and Jack.

5 Months Previously...

Whilst sitting enjoying a drink in a local boozer, he had spotted a face he thought he recognised from the past. Sitting in the corner were two middle aged women, one big busty and blonde, the other slim with red hair. Their years of drinking, telling on their faces. Amused at this turn of events and brimming with confidence due to the alcohol he had consumed, he walked over to the table where the women sat. When he approached the table both women looked up from their conversation.

"Kathy? It is you...isn't it?" They both stared at him bewildered, as to this stranger's identity. It was the big blonde one who spoke first, "Who wants to know?" She answered, slurring her words. Tony knew right away it was her, once he heard her voice, nice to see she had not changed, still liked her drink.

"Tony...Tony Davis! You might remember me better as Fran's other half!" The smile fell from her face, she remembered him alright, He had chased Fran until she eventually gave into him. At the time it suited Fran, as she had just confided in her that she was pregnant and did not want to be on her own. After Fran had given birth to her daughter, Kathy had watched her friend's demise from a sociable, chatty, fun-loving person into a recluse. Although Fran was still enjoying a drink, she was very rarely out in the local pubs, so she and Tony preferred to stay at home drinking. As the years went by, she had tried to get through to Fran, offering her help with the baby but it was always declined. Until eventually they both parted ways as good friends.

"Ah right, I hardly recognised you there. Are you two still together then? I haven't seen Fran in years!"

"Sometimes Aye sometimes naw!" He laughed, "We have three kids. They kind of keep us together, if you know what I mean. I couldn't not be there for them," he boasted, puffing his chest outwards. "That's right, the last time I saw Fran she was pregnant. That must have been with your first boy then?"

Moving around the table, he pulled up a seat and sat down next to Kathy.

"My first boy Brian, we have Ian as well…"

"That's right! And how is wee Lena doing? She'll be getting up now as well. That's good of you to bring the wee lassie up as yours Tony, says alot about a man that can bring up another man's child." The moment the words had left her lips, Kathy knew from the look on his face that she had put her foot in it!

Bloody hell…He didn't know!

The moment those words registered in his mind, was the beginning of the end for him and Fran. There would be no coming back from this for them!

Every day thereafter, all he heard were those words '**other man's child**'. It played on his mind twenty four hours a day. He had managed to keep his meeting with Kathy to himself for four days. Fran had no idea that he had met

Kathy, or the secret she had mistakenly divulged to him, until eventually that night when they had both been drinking heavily for hours.

"Hey, you'll never guess who I bumped into the other night!"
Fran lay on the couch, swinging her half empty glass of wine, her foot tapping to the sound of The Waterboys playing in the background. "Well, I'm not a bloody psychic! Who? Surprise me!"
Oh, I'll surprise you alright, he thought. "Your old friend Kathy!" He watched the recognition register on her face, "You remember her, don't you? She has not changed one bit, still a drunken old cow! In fact, she was that drunk she let one of your secrets out! Didn't mean to...It just came out...Any idea which one? I'm sure you two shared many!"

Fran heard the menace in his voice and sat upright against the cushions, "I've no idea what you're on about!" Across the room Tony could feel the rage build up inside of him, "Really! Would you like me to remind you? Wait! Let me give you a clue...Lena!"
"What about Lena?"
He had to work really hard at containing the urge to grab her by the hair and slap the truth out of her, "DON'T play me for a fucking idiot anymore Fran! You know fine well what I'm on about, so spill!"
"I don't! What do you mean Lena? She doesn't even know Lena!" She was pleading now. She had an idea what this was about, she had

agonised about the truth coming out over the years.

Standing, she slowly made her way over to where Tony was standing, taking his hand in hers she knelt before him, "Tony, I haven't seen her for years, how would she know Lena or anything about us? She was always trying to cause trouble with us, I think she's jealous of what we have! Don't let her drunken stories get to you!"
At that moment he lost it! Grabbing Fran by the neck he pulled her up onto her feet, "**DON'T! JUST DON'T!** I've had enough of your lies to last a feckin lifetime...**She told me! I know Lena's not mine Fran! SO, WHO IS HE**?"

As much as Fran tried to explain her actions and apologise for betraying him, she would not tell him who had got her pregnant and it was not helping the situation. He exploded, with all of the built up rage he had been carrying around in him for days resulting in the massive fight and Fran ending up in a hospital bed.

When he walked out that night after the fight, he really had no idea where he was going. The one thing he knew for certain was that he would find out the identity of Lena's father and make him pay!

That night he had slept in a shop doorway, down a back alley in the centre of town. In the morning, he awoke feeling cold, tired, and angry. He had not slept much, his head was throbbing, he had a plan though to help him find the answer he was seeking. He would go back to the pub where he had last seen Kathy and get to the truth of the matter from her. It was the least she could do, she owed him that much after dropping such a bombshell!

Luckily for him, he did not need to wait long to find Kathy again, the first night he struck gold. He sat at the bar sipping a pint; he had found enough change in his pocket for one, he had to make this drink last. Just after seven in the evening, the pub doors opened and in walked Kathy with the same friend she had been with before.

He waited until they had been served with their drinks and found a seat. Warily, he walked towards noticing the change in Kathy's facial expression the minute she saw him. After she dropped the bombshell on him the previous time they had met, she refused to answer any questions he put to her. It was obvious to him that although she had meant no harm, she still had a loyalty towards Fran, he knew he would need every ounce of patience to get the information he wanted. He felt sure she knew who fathered Lena and he had no intention of letting her go this time...not until she told him!

When he discovered that Lena was not his biological daughter, then later finding out that she was in fact Jack's, he was distraught. He felt cheated and used, at the extent of Fran's lies and deceit through all those years, he was angry seeking revenge.

CHAPTER TWENTY-TWO

Sylvie unlocked the front door and crept into the hallway as quietly as she could. It was the early hours of the morning, she presumed Jack would be asleep in bed upstairs, having drunk himself into a stupor, how wrong she was.
She had removed her high heels at the front door and carried them in her arms, popping her head into the living room. She was surprised to find him slouched on the sofa, empty glass in hand, staring into space.

"You took your time! Wasn't sure you would have the nerve to show your face!" There was a hint of menace in his tone.
"I thought you would be in bed sleeping. I was going to use one of the spare bedrooms so that I would not disturb you!" She knew she would need to try and play to his better nature, he did have one, although he did not show it very often.

Jack gave a sarcastic laugh, "Yeah, yeah very good Sylvie! There's no way you're getting out of this one! So, you can get your arse over here and start explaining!"

The atmosphere in the room was thick with fraught. Keeping her eyes firmly fixed on the cream carpet, she slowly walked over to the opposite sofa from where he sat and tentatively sat down.

"Jack! It is not what you think! I was passing by and saw Tony going into the container, I wanted to see what he was up to! "

Getting up from the sofa, Jack walked towards her, "Really? You honestly think I am that stupid? Try again love!"

Standing in front of her, she could not ignore how rugged and handsome he looked, even more so when he was angry. Yet she had to remind herself of the danger she was facing, keeping herself in one piece was the most important thing right now!

"It is the truth! You don't think I'm that desperate surely? Even if he was the last man on earth, I'd never go near him! You must know that?" Aware of the panic in her voice, she stopped herself. If he sensed that she was scared it would be game over for her!

"Honestly Sylv I don't know what to think right now! I do know you've been acting way out of your usual ways... That's a fact! How do you even know him? If you ain't shacking up with him, what other reason could there possibly be for you two to be in touch?"

Time was moving on, the morning light was breaking through the living room windows, Sylvie's adrenaline diminished, she was exhausted, in dire need of her bed, yet she could not stop Jack's bombardment of questions from coming her way. It was only a matter of time before she cracked and told him the truth!

"Alright...Alright! It was Tony that got in touch with me, somehow, he found out where you lived, he has been following us both." With her mind working overtime, she was trying to tell him without endangering herself more. "He stopped me in the street outside the nail salon, told me had to speak to me ... like it was really urgent! At first, I didn't even know he was your brother, I was shocked when he said 'cause you've always said he was dead! Then I thought there was something wrong with you, so I listened to what he had to say..."

***That sounds plausible*!** Hoping this would pacify him for the moment, give her time to think up valid reasons for her being with Tony. "Jack I'm knackered! I really need some sleep... Please?"

"Good try Sylv, we've only just begun, you've got a lot more explaining than that to do doll! What was so important that he had to tell you? Once you tell me that wee nugget, then you can go catch your beauty sleep! Until then you ain't going nowhere!"

Knowing he meant what he said, Sylvie sat back on the sofa to make herself comfortable. It was going to be a long night...

"He told me he wanted to meet up with you again. Wanted me to facilitate a meeting for you both. I was surprised he wanted to see you again, I've been worrying how to tell you, that's why I've been acting weird! I went today to tell him I would ask you... Nothing else to it!"

"So, why was he wanting to meet me now? It's not adding up Sylv... You need to try telling me the truth here. Has he got anything to do with the deal going to shit?"

"I don't think so... How would he know anything about your business dealings? "She was panicking, had to put him off track, or she would never see the full light of day again.

Jack did not believe what she had told him, she was lying, he felt it in his gut. He would wait until the morning then ask her more questions, perhaps it would require more force to get to the truth, it was up to Sylvie just how forceful he would be!

CHAPTER TWENTY-THREE

The pain in Fran's back was bad today. It was radiating down her legs so she decided today would be a rest day; this entailed resting and taking the medications to help reduce inflammation and pain, try, and get on top of it again. Once she was up on her feet and working the exercise programme she had been given at the hospital, she felt that there was light at the end of the tunnel regarding living with pain. However, she was quickly reminded that if she did not pace herself, then she would pay for it! Due to her personality and 'can do' attitude it was becoming a never ending circle of severe to moderate pain daily. Mentally, she was struggling, but she kept this as hidden as she could. The last thing her kids, especially Lena, needed right now was her having a melt down!

Lying on the sofa with a hot water bottle at the base of her back, watching daytime tv, Fran worried about the situation she had found herself and family in with Jack and Tony. Deep down inside she knew it was not going to end well. Experience of both men told her to expect more fireworks, they had never gotten along, now with her secret exposed, they were both capable of dangerous underhand play. Her main concern was that she and her family would not become collateral damage!

Just as the afternoon news was starting, she heard the front door bang close. In walked Brian with his head down, "Why aren't you at school?" Enquired Fran, "I'm not going back there! Not ever!" Came his reply, as he made his way towards the chair opposite from where she lay. "Why what's happening now? You can't just walk out from school Son..."

"I just have, and I mean it, I'm not going back there, I hate everyone in it!" Fran took a deep breath, this was all she needed today of all days! Looking across at her boy, she could sense his hurt, she saw it on his face. "Right...What's happened? Tell me the truth now I won't be angry." Slowly, she moved herself into a more comfortable upright position from where she lay, the pain was becoming a little more bearable with the help of her tablets.

"When I went in this morning everything was ok until Marcus Reilly appeared. He started slagging me off about Dad."
"That's nothing new surely? The whole town knows he's a good for nothing drunk at the best of times, sure he is always disappearing and coming back, don't bother yourself with that nonsense now!" Fran was trying desperately to deescalate the situation as fast as she could. Brian began shaking his head in disagreement, "It's not that...He says he overheard his Mum and her friend talking about Dad. Says he's left us and has been staying with his mum's friend because he found something out..."

Oh, dear lord!

Fran's blood ran cold through her. Sitting herself up against the support cushion she used, Fran remained neutral faced, praying Brian was not going to say what she had feared all this time!

"Who found something out?"
Brian looked straight at her, "My Dad. Marcus says Dad found out that he's not really our dad! Says I don't know who my real Dad is! He's told the whole play yard at school...I'm never going back there; they were all laughing at me!" Tears began to fall down his cheeks. "Come here," she said, tapping beside her on the sofa. It was times like this when she wished her mobility were better, she wanted to rush over to where he sat crying, throw her arms around him to reassure him.

Reluctantly, Brian came over and knelt down at her side. Placing her arms around him, "Don't listen to them Brian, they don't know a thing! That Marcus boy has listened all wrong. Your Dad is YOUR Dad, whether we like it or not! "She was trying to throw a little light on the situation by using humour, however, it was not making her boy laugh.

What the hell, I'm going to have to explain this to him now!

Nervously, she began stroking Brian's hair, "Listen to what I'm going to tell you and know that THIS is the truth! Your Dad IS your DAD! He is and always will be! This boy Marcus has misunderstood what his mum was saying."

"But he says Dad's been living with this other woman because of you and us!" The tears began to flow from his eyes once more.

"He left because of me! Nothing at all to do with you, your brother or Lena. It was something between me and your dad!"

Fran stopped stroking his hair, turned his face upwards, so that she was looking him straight in the eyes.

"Brian, your dad left because he discovered something I hadn't told him a long time ago. When I met your dad, I was already expecting Lena!" She could not get any other words out, "SO, it is TRUE! He is not our dad!"

"Brian calm down! He is your dad! Yours and Ian's! He's just not Lena's biological father, but he is still her dad, because he has always been there for her too!" He pulled away from her.

Inside Fran's heart was aching, she saw the pain and confusion written over her boy's face. This was her worst nightmare, right here in this very moment, she had to find a way to make him understand her position without it pulling them apart!

"Before I met your dad, I was pregnant, I didn't say anything to your dad at the time, and for that I am wrong, I should have been truthful! The honest truth is that I knew your Uncle Jack before I had even met your dad, I did not know they were related, as neither of them mentioned the other one…" Fran hesitated, unsure how to carry on with her explanation.

"So, Uncle Jack's Lena's Dad? "Brian looked as shocked as he sounded.

Fran's heart was racing, "Yes, he is! Lena has only found this out herself recently, she had no idea. "Son, we love you! This stuff is for me and your dad to sort out. He is still your dad and I am still your Mum, that is something which will never change! Lena is still your sister too!" Brian got up from the floor, walked silently over to the chair once more. "Brian, say something please…" She pleaded. He remained silent and looked deep in thought.

Fran decided to leave him be. He needed time to digest what she had just told him. Time would tell if he believed her, she prayed he would.

"Hey Mum, we're back! Could not see Brian at the school gates so I only picked this one up as I was passing that way today." In walked Lena with Ian in tow.

JEEZUS! Fran could not help but wonder what was coming next, this day was becoming her living nightmare!

Forcing a smile onto her face, she turned, just as Brian found his voice again. "Oh, Hi Sister!" He called out sarcastically. Fran turned to face him, giving him a warning glare not to push it any further.

"Why are you here already, were you not at school this afternoon?" Asked Lena. She could sense an atmosphere in the living room but was unsure of what she had walked into again.

"I've left that place and I'm not going back, we are all a laughing stock and I'm not going to take it no more, I don't have to!" Lena laughed loudly, "Who poked your cage?" Continuing to laugh, she walked into the kitchen.

"YOU! You are the reason!" Brian's raised voice shocked them all. Ian sat on the sofa next to his mum and snuggled deeper into her as Brian continued shouting at Lena.

Lena stepped out of the kitchen, walked over to where Brian remained seated, "What is your problem with me today then? Go ahead, fill me in!" Rage was written all over her face, as Fran looked on; for the first time she noticed a similarity to Jack, as she watched Lena confront Brian.

"Out with it! What have I meant to have done to upset you so much today then? You were fine when you left this morning, so what happened?" Her anger began to subside when she saw tears of frustration fall from her brothers' face.

"Right, that's enough you two!" Fran would not allow them to rip into one another, they had to stick together.

Lena's stare remained firmly fixed on Brian.

"He knows Lena! He knows everything!" Fran quietly stated.

Lena turned to look at her mum, who was cuddling Ian, whilst nodding her head, "Some boy at school overheard gossip..." Brian looked up at her. Recognising the enormity of the situation for him, she bent forward and took her brother into her arms, as tears fell from both their eyes.

CHAPTER TWENTY-FOUR

Sylvie woke up to the smell of freshly brewed coffee coming from the kitchen across the hallway. Last night she was exhausted, so decided to sleep on the sofa in the lounge room, rather than try to get into her bed next to Jack. It would only have ended up causing more trouble between them both. As the memories from the previous night began swirling around in her mind, she brought the blanket up over her head, today could wait, she was not ready for the inquisition from Jack today!

"Wakey! Wakey!" Jack had entered the lounge and was standing above her. Pulling the blanket closer to her face Sylvie tried to ignore him, however, this was not working, as the next thing she felt was him nudging her body, "C'mon sleeping beauty, think I've forgotten about last night? No chance! Get yourself up Sylvie before I drag you up!"

Shit! He will not give up!

Eventually, she raised herself up from the sofa, dreading what was coming next. "I'm just going to freshen up…I'll be back down in five minutes!" Thinking this would allow her some time to collect her thoughts and come up with a reasonable excuse for her being in the same vicinity as Tony, she was wrong!

"Never mind freshening up! Get your arse in here now, I've gone to all the trouble of making you a coffee, now you can do me the honour of joining me and speaking the truth! This isn't going away Sylv!" There was malice in the way he spoke to her, her heart was racing as she walked through to join him at the breakfast bar in the kitchen.

The smell of the coffee was strangely comforting to her. Sitting across from her Jack looked self-assured, dressed in his designer suit trousers with a fresh crisp white shirt. She had to give it to him, he never allowed himself to look anything other than fashionably dressed, there was also the aroma of one of his many designer aftershaves, he meant business this morning. Meanwhile Sylvie had yet to wash or change her clothes from the previous day, he already had the upper hand before anything was spoken.

"I have no intention of wasting my morning, so get on with it!"
With her stomach in knots, she sat opposite him with her head down, whether she told him the truth or lied, she decided either way she was done for.
 "Jack, seriously I told you everything last night, there is nothing else to add and I'm not going to

sit here and make something up just to make you feel better! "

"BETTER! BETTER? You actually think there's anything you can say that will make this situation better...Seriously? If you think for a minute there is, then you're even thicker than I thought you were before all this shit!" The anger was visible across his face, he got up and began pacing back and forwards in front of her.

"Sylv, all I want from you is the truth! Why are you finding it so bloody hard to tell me...Eh?

"She shook her head, "The more you say what you're saying is the truth, it is just making me question it more, 'cause I aint feckin stupid, I know you and believe me I know him! I've never spoken about Tony to you for a reason. The reason being I don't want him in my life! So...Why were you meeting up with him?"

"I've told you! He wanted to get in touch with you through me! Nothing more, nothing less! Okay, I should have told you straight away when he stopped me that day in the street, but I thought I would find out exactly what he wanted from you before I said. You've been that stressed lately because of the deal going wrong. I was only looking out for you...Stupid me for thinking about you! "Eventually, stopping to take a breather, she began silently praying he would accept her reasoning and she could get on with her day.

He was still pacing the room with his hands in his trouser pockets, head down, shaking it from side to side, "I still don't believe one word you're saying, I can feel it in my gut that you're lying! When I find out...AND I WILL FIND OUT THE TRUTH...You and him are gonna pay big time, mark my words!" Suddenly, he stopped walking back and forth, "You had better watch yourself Sylv 'cause you're playing a dangerous game, and you are well out of your depths!" With the threat still in the air, he turned his back and walked away from her.

Getting up from the breakfast bar she walked slowly into the hallway where she watched him grab his suit jacket and leave the house. Closing her eyes, she let out a big sigh of relief, for the time being.

Once in his car Jack punched the steering wheel with rage. He had felt it building up inside him as he listened to her make her feeble excuses to him. Pulling out from the driveway, he knew it was only a matter of time before he found out exactly what the pair of them were up to behind his back.

He had put Daz on the case to follow Tony from the moment he had left them both in the container on the wasteland. Earlier that morning, he had taken a call from Daz, who had already found some disturbing evidence showing the extent of their deceit. Racing towards the city centre to meet Daz, he would take on board what he had found out, then he would decide what actions to take against them both!

CHAPTER TWENTY-FIVE

Traffic heading into Glasgow was extremely busy for the time of day. It allowed Jack time to calm down, to start thinking more clearly. There were elements of what Sylvie had said that he could not shake from his mind. When she had said that

Tony just appeared out of the blue one day, he found this at least to be true. What was not sitting easily with him was why. Why would he be looking to stroll back into his life now? It was not because he had fallen on hard times and was looking for money from him. Tony was always aware of his brother's lifestyle, surely if he needed anything he would have been in touch long before now. No! There had to be something much more at stake than money...Then suddenly, like a lightning bolt, it hit him...Lena!

Elated that he had worked it all out before his meeting with Daz, he smiled to himself, before the realisation hit him...

HE'S TOLD HER!

Stuck in the traffic jam, he was astonished that he had never given it a second thought, regarding the possibility of Tony telling Sylvie he had fathered Lena. Never had he considered the thought of Sylvie finding out, especially from Tony of all people. His concentration was broken by the gradual movement of traffic ahead of him, allowing him to continue on with his quest to meet Daz.

They had arranged to meet up in The Bay Horse pub right in the centre of Glasgow on Bath Street, within easy walking distance to other watering holes, thus allowing them to make collections from punters after their meeting. Jack was still having cash flow problems, the result of the

botched drug deal, it was now public knowledge that someone had gotten one over on him, this was not helping them in their pursuit to cash in. He found Daz sitting on a barstool at the corner of the bar. "What are you having?" Daz asked, nodding towards the bar. "Guiness and a whisky chaser," ... You been here long then?" Jack noticed the empty pint glass in front of Daz. "Yeah, just had to get out the house, the missus was giving me earache,"
Jack laughed, "You and I both mate! Here grab a seat in that booth. I'll wait for my drink."

When they were settled Jack looked around the bar area, "Not many folks around here, is there? Or are they hiding from us?" Laughing, he then took a sip of the golden liquid in his glass, he felt the burn at the back of his throat, which he savoured.

"So...What's the information you've got for me? "

Daz placed his pint on the table in front of him, "You had better steady yourself Boss! I've been tailing Tony as you asked, nothing unusual really, he basically goes from pub to pub until his luck runs out and nobody buys him a drink. I was beginning to get a bit bored to be honest with you, then..." He stopped to take a drink of his pint, "Right, get on with it!" Urged Jack. "Well, I was following him for a few days, same pubs on different days like...The old guy behind the bar in Lauders catches sight of me watching your man, when Tony goes to the toilet the old guy waves me over. Obviously, he knows who I am and who I work for. He's saying he is not looking for trouble in his bar and I'm reassuring him there isn't going to be any. I tell him I'm just watching your man to see if he meets anyone, he shouldn't be...right, this is where it gets interesting Boss! He tells me your man has met with a well turned-out blonde woman several times in his bar, pointing to the booth where they sit. I ask him to describe her in more detail and he only goes and tells me he can do one better...He has security footage!! "Beaming from ear to ear, Daz continues, "I tell him I want to see it, so he takes me through the back to his office and shows me one of the meetups...Boss, it's your Sylvie!"

Jack throws the remains of his whisky down his throat in one.

"It's all making sense now! The dirty lying bitch! How many times did he say they met up?"
Looking at Daz, Jack saw confusion written all over his face...
" You knew? You have had me spending my days and nights following that piece of shit and you've known, all this time!"
Shaking his head from side-to-side Jack replied, "No, I never knew a thing until I was driving in here to meet you today. It all came to me when I was thinking about Sylvie's excuses for being with him! She kept saying he just turned up, this kept turning in my head. When I asked myself why he would just turn up out of the blue, it came to me...He was telling her about Lena!"

Daz appeared more confused. He had no knowledge of Jack's sexual relationship with Fran; therefore, he was shocked when Jack brought him up to date with everything which had happened in his private life recently.

They spent the next hour going through all the details they had uncovered between watching Tony and what Jack had disclosed. Daz had many questions which Jack felt obliged to answer, after all the man had always been there for him in times of need. He was mindful this was certainly his time of need, it was vital he had Daz's loyalty, as it was becoming more apparent, he did not have many loyal people around him.

Taking another gulp of his drink Daz stopped and turned to face him, "Boss, there's something missing here... Okay, so he tells Sylvie about you being Lena's real Dad?" Jack nodded, "Right, so what's he hoping to get out of it then? I mean, he hasn't been trying to blackmail you for cash. So, he tells her, then what? She hasn't let a peep out that she knows either. I think they're both up to something else Boss!" Jack looked lost in thought, " I think your right mate! It would not have taken them all those meetings to tell her about Lena. I've a feeling they could be meddling in my business. If I find out for sure that they're behind the botched deal, I'll kill them myself!" Inside, Jack's stomach was lurching at the idea of Sylvie betraying him in this manner, however, he would not hesitate in teaching her a deadly lesson if he discovered she was indeed involved in trying to bring him down!

CHAPTER TWENTY-SIX

It was a lovely warm sunny morning in Glasgow, the bonus for Lena was that it was also Saturday, which meant she did not have to worry about getting the boys organised for school. Both boys had stayed over with their friend Barry along the street, it had been planned, due to it being the boy's birthday.

Today, she had decided to go into town for a look at the shops. Jack had given her and the boys some money the last time he had been at the flat checking in on them all. It felt good having money in her purse for her to buy whatever her heart desired for once, she was so used to scrimping and saving in order to buy anything new, having Jack in their lives did have its benefits. Sitting brushing her hair upon her bed, she could hear her mum's footsteps coming up the hallway. In the past few weeks, she had watched her mum become more independent and slightly more mobile, she was learning that pacing herself was the main priority in managing her pain levels. It was clear to see that her mum was in a better place, although she still had good and bad days.

 "You're there! Did you not hear me shouting?" Popping her head around the bedroom door, Fran seemed agitated. "Obviously, I never heard you or I would have answered you! What's wrong?" Looking forward to her day out, Lena was in no mood for drama of any kind, not today! Fran shifted the door further open, so that she could see her daughter fully.
"It's that eejit your dad! I haven't heard a word from him, and he owes me money..." Fran saw Lena roll her eyes, "And don't you bother with any attitude missy! |"
"You should have known better than to give him money. You know he'll only drink it." Lena had already second guessed her mum, she realised the moment she was complaining about having no money, she was after hers. **No chance!**

"Mum, I don't know what you expect me to do about him. I haven't seen him and don't really want to if truth be said! I don't have any money to give you either! You shouldn't have given him anything, especially after the way he's treated you and us, he doesn't deserve anything!" Lena could feel the hurt and anger build up inside, they were bubbling underneath, she prayed her mum would not push the conversation any further, she was ready to explode.

One day! Just one day away from all this! It's not too much to ask for, is it?
Reluctantly, she admitted it was! Feeling deflated and just as she was about to offer her spending money to her mum, there was banging on the front door.

"Fran! Fran! Come quick!" More banging, "Fran! Hurry, it's your Tony...Quick!"
Lena ran down the hallway, whilst Fran followed behind her. Upon opening the front door, they were surprised to find old Mrs Taggart from up the road, looking aghast.
"What's the emergency? What's going on?" Asked Fran, her heart racing in anticipation of the woman's answer.
"Fran, Lena, you had better come fast! Tony's been found lying in the undergrowth behind the flats...I think it's bad, so you two had better brace yourselves! The Police and ambulance are there now! "Mrs Taggart turned and ran down the stairs, Fran and Lena followed behind her.

When they reached the end of the street there was already a throng of bystanders. As they pushed their way through, they could see the Police cars and an ambulance with the door open but no one in it. Looking at one another they both feared the worst.

"Mum, you should go tell the Police who you are, see if they will tell you what's happened." Fran's heart was racing so fast she felt as though she was going to pass out. "Excuse me! Excuse me!" Making her way past all the onlookers. Eventually, she reached the front of the crowd, "Excuse me! "She called out to a Policeman, who was standing next to the cordoned off area. "Excuse me! Can you tell me what's happened please? I've been told that's my man! Can you let me know please!" The police officer walked over towards her, "What's your name? "He asked, "Fran Davis. I have been told that's my man Tony Davis. Something has happened to him; will you tell me what is going on please?" She was pleading with him for information.

"I'm sorry I can't tell you anything at the moment, the person has not been identified yet." Fran felt her legs give way as his words hit her, she fell to the ground below her.

"Mum! Mum!" Lena watched her mum ask the officer then fall down. As fast as she could, she pushed her way through the onlookers until eventually she reached where her mum lay. "Mum, what did he say?" Trying to help her mum to her feet, "Mum, what is it?" Looking up, the Policeman came to assist her, "What did you tell her? Is it my dad? Is he dead? "The Officer managed to get Fran up onto her feet again, "Listen...I can't tell you any more than a body was discovered, as yet we don't know who it is but if it's your dad then someone will be in touch, until then please try and look after yourselves."

Fran sobbed uncontrollably, Lena placed her arms around her shoulders, "Mum, we don't know for sure it's Dad. Let's get you home and see if the Police come with news." Fear and dread coursing through her body and mind, Lena guided her mum back home to wait and see if what everyone around them was saying was to be the truth!

CHAPTER TWENTY-SEVEN

The moment they returned home Lena gently sat her mum on the sofa, "There, sit here and I'll go make us a nice cuppa tea, try not to worry Mum. Worry when worry comes eh?" Aware that the words she was saying were not how she was feeling inside. When she was standing in the crowd waiting on Fran asking the Police what was going on, Lena heard the rumours which were racing all around her. The main one being that it was indeed her dad who had been found in the long grasses behind the tenement building, apparently, he had been stabbed to death.

The noise of the kettle boiling brought her mind back into the kitchen. Unsure of how she was feeling, Lena went about making tea, taking it into the living room where her mum sat staring into space.

"Here Mum, take a sip of tea, it'll help calm you. You're in shock!" Fran's gaze broke from the wall as she stared at Lena. "And, what about you...Are you in shock? Cause you don't seem to be bothered if it is him lying up there!" There was spite in her words, Lena remained standing in front of her, "We don't even know for sure it is him yet! "The atmosphere was broken by knocking at the front door, "It is him! That's them here to tell us..." Fran fell back against the sofa, with her face in her hands, dread coursing through her body whilst tears fell as she sobbed.

Once the Officers had left, Lena had to give Fran some medication to calm her down. When the Officer informed them that it was indeed Tony Davis that had been discovered lying stabbed in the undergrowth, Fran had gone hysterical, crying, and screaming. Lena convinced the police that she would be okay to be left with her mum as her uncle would be over soon. Although they needed the body to be formally identified, the officers were sure it was Tony, he was known to them, due to his drinking escapades. They left a card with contact details, gave their sincere sympathies then left. It was only when she was on her own Lena felt the enormity of the situation hit her, emotionally exhausted, tears rolled down her cheeks.

As the news spread around the street, it wasn't long before Brian and Ian returned asking questions. Both boys broke down and cried when Lena explained what had happened to their dad. The pressure was heavy upon Lena, she was worried about the impact this would have on her brothers, along with how her mum was going to cope. The last thing she needed was for her mum to start drowning her sorrows with the drink once more. Tears began to form in her eyes, as she tried to blink them away, the living room door opened, "I've just heard..."
It was Jack.

Upon entering the room, seeing Lena with tears in her eyes, Jack opened his arms, "Come here you...You don't need to do this alone anymore you know!" Gradually, Lena got up from the chair, tears poured down her face when she walked into his embrace. Sobbing, she allowed all the emotions she had been holding onto out, for the first time, she felt safe in his arms.
Jack cradled his daughter, seeing that for once he was providing her with a degree of comfort. He felt a connection with her in that moment, he admitted to himself that it felt good having her so close. He looked over to where both boys sat crying, trying to hide their emotions behind cushions, "Come here you two," opening his

embrace, he invited the boys in along with their sister, Brian and Ian ran into his arms. In that moment he felt a great sense of responsibility for the three of them, silently he promised to them and himself that whatever may happen in the future, he would be there for them.

Eventually, Fran surfaced from her bed later that evening. Jack had bought them all a takeaway for their dinner as no one was up to cooking. Unsurprisingly, most of the takeaway went into the bin, apart from Ian, the others did not have much of an appetite. The sound of the television was the only noise in the living room where they all sat. The atmosphere tense, "Lena, will you take the boys into their rooms please? I need to talk to your Mum." Getting up from where they sat, Lena ushered the boys through to their bedrooms.

"What do the coppers think happened to him then?" He was aware the police would be wanting to speak with him, probably asking where he was the night before, he was well prepared with his answers, it came with the territory.
"They haven't said anything about that yet. They've only just found him! Do you know anything about it? Was it you?" Before the calming medication took effect earlier, Fran had lay wondering what had happened to Tony. She was not naive enough to think it was a random attack, she understood he had quite a few enemies, people he had wronged one way or another. With the idea that Jack could be

involved swirling around her mind, her stomach began churning, her anxiety levels were at an all time high. Facing him now, she believed him when he denied any knowledge about Tony's untimely death.

"If it wasn't you, then who do you think did it then?"

Jack shrugged his shoulders, "No idea...I mean let's be honest we both know he had wronged a lot of people Fran. Take your pick! The one thing is the old bill will be all over this, they'll soon get whoever it was." Noticing how anxious she seemed, he tried to sway her fears, "You don't have anything to worry about,"
"How can you be so sure? What if whoever did this to him, comes for me or the kids? I won't be able to relax until they catch who murdered him...I'm scared!"

CHAPTER TWENTY-EIGHT

Inside The Horse & Cart the atmosphere was relaxed, the soft background music added to the ambience of the place, much to the delight of the evening crowd. Sitting in a booth, looking out onto Renfield Street, were Kathy and her friend Maria all set for a night of boozing and frolics.

"You fancy a change Kathy, what about a wee cocktail? We deserve a treat!" Maria shimmied along the seat, until she eventually stood at the side of the table.

"Aye, alright go on then! You still have some cash on you?"

Smiling, Maria nodded, "I'll choose...surprise you, right!" Kathy laughed at her friend's spontaneity; it was amazing what a bit of extra money could do to change a person's mood.

As she sat watching Maria trying to get served at the bar, Kathy had no regrets about telling the two men that had appeared the previous week of Tony Davis's whereabouts. At first sight of them, she was terrified, they were big and burly in stature, with an air of danger around them. Right away, she knew they were trouble with a capital T!

When they forced their way into her home, she had feared for her life. However, they quickly informed her that she was in no danger, as long as she informed them where they could find Tony Davis.

Apparently, they had been looking for him for some time with no luck of his whereabouts. Kathy knew exactly where he was hiding but was not sure she wanted to divulge that information to them. The moment one of the guys had mentioned that there would be a monetary reward for information, it was not long until Kathy was on the phone to Maria telling her to come round right away!

"Hey! What are you sitting there mulling over? I can see the wee mouse on the wheel from here!" Maria laughed, returning to the booth, carrying a tray of colourful cocktails for them both.

"Uch, nothing much! I was just wondering if they guys found Tony and hoping they didn't do too much damage to him! Do you not feel a bit guilty giving them his whereabouts, I mean you and him were meant to be in love?"
Maria positioned herself once more behind the table, reaching over for her cocktail glass. She was laughing, "Naw, he was a lousy lover, and my house is cleaner without him staying in it as well. You know he is one filthy git! Pity he wasn't like that in the bedroom I might not have daubed him in!" The pair's laughter could be heard over the soft music in the bar.

The evening continued with more cocktails and laughter, until Kathy saw a face, she recognised standing at the bar all alone. Thinking that tonight may be her night, she approached the guy, trying hard to walk in a straight line.

"Well, hello! If it isn't Mr Jack Davis's right-hand man himself!" She was aware how much of her cleavage she was showing, she had pulled her top down as she made her way over in his direction, men could not resist her ample cleavage.

Turning to face her, she watched with delight, just as his eyes dropped to take in her bust before looking up at her face.

"Sorry Love, I think you've got the wrong fella!" Daz replied, he was well aware who was standing next to him, he had heard her before he had seen her when he first entered the bar, he recognised her straight away. He just wanted to enjoy his pint in peace.

"No, I have not! It's me Daz, Kathy Semple! You must remember me and Fran. We used to drink in The Basement Club, that was where we first met you and Jack."
Given the news which Jack had told him regards when he had first met Fran, he was not sure whether he wanted to continue chatting with this woman or not. It quickly became apparent to him that he was not getting a choice!

Moving closer to where he stood, Kathy could smell his aftershave, *Gosh,he smells good!*
"My friend is sitting just over there," she said pointing in the direction of Maria. "Why don't

you buy us both a drink and come over to join the party?" She sensed his hesitance, "Come on! A drink for old times' sake..." Placing her arm under his, she gently nudged him in the direction of their booth.

Realising he was not going to get peace until he had bought them a drink, Daz gave into her demands, following behind her to where Maria sat waiting. "Look who has come to join us!" Kathy called out as she approached the table, "This is Maria...Maria this is my old friend Daz, we go way back...Don't we Daz?" Nervously, Daz sat whilst nodding his head, "Aye way back. Listen...I'm only in for a quiet drink so I'll leave these here for you to enjoy." Placing the glasses on the table he tried to return back to the bar, but Kathy was having none of it, forcing him to take a seat opposite Maria.

A half hour later he had heard enough nonsense about how her life had been since their last encounter. "Right ladies, as much as I've enjoyed our wee catch up through the years, it's time I was heading home. My missus will be wondering where I've got to!"
"But wait, you've not told me how Jack is doing or if any of you see Fran these days!" She had to find out if what she had told Tony the last time, she had spoken to him had gotten back to Fran in any way.

Daz found himself unsure what to reply to her question, "Yeah, I see Jack as you know. He has been in touch with Fran recently, due to what happened to Tony, she's needed support, it's tough for her." Thinking he had played it safe with his reply, until he noticed the colour drain from both the faces sitting across the table from him.

"What do you mean...What's happened to Tony?" Panic rising within her, it was Maria who asked the question.

Daz got up to make his exit, "Did you not hear? He was stabbed to death last week. They found his body at the weekend!" With that said, he thanked them both, but not before noticing the shock and awkward glances that passed between the two women.

CHAPTER TWENTY-NINE

Frans pain levels were at an all-time high of late. The stress of Tony's death, arranging his funeral and the house being busy with a constant stream of people wanting to show their condolences, was taking its toll on not only her, but them all.

Both the boys had taken his death really badly, nothing surprising, as they adorned him. They had taken to spending a lot of time in their bedroom, not wanting to be amongst the visitors, she understood this. If she had the choice, she would spend her time hiding underneath her duvet cover in bed. This was not an option, so every day she tried her best to hide her pain, both physically and mentally. It was becoming harder to hide, due to the fact she had not been pacing herself properly, doing too much, her back was stiffening up with all the tension. Fran was becoming annoyed with herself at her lack of independence, whilst she relied upon Lena again and again.

"Lena love, I'm going to lie down for an hour. Is that okay with you? You can always wake me if someone comes to the door."
Lena had been sitting writing a to-do list. There was so much needing to be done after Tony's funeral, it was never ending. The Police were still in contact on a regular basis, keeping them up to date with their enquiries. They were also asking if any of the well-wishers had dropped any new

information that they had heard on the streets. So far, there had been nothing new to tell them.

"That's fine Mum, wait and I'll give you a hand," Lena placed her writing pad on the table, before helping Fran onto her feet and walking alongside her holding her arm.

"Soon hopefully, all this will be dealt with Mum, and we can get back to some kind of normality. You will need to try to slow down or you're going to end up with more muscle spasms. We don't like seeing you in so much pain, please let Uncle Jack deal with more things, he doesn't mind!"

"I will...To be honest my body is not giving me the choice anymore; it's screaming at me to rest! The pain is unbearable, like a burning pain, I feel as though my spine's a hot poker!" Stated Fran, falling on top of her bed. "Just leave me like this, I don't want to feel like this, Lena. You and your brothers have too much to cope with as it is. It's not fair!" Fran began crying. Lena moved around to the other side of the bed and lay down next to her mum. Placing her arms gently around her, "Mum, please don't get upset. You'll rest and take the meds, then you will be back up with us. There is nothing else we can do. Uncle Jack is popping in later, I'll show him the things which still need doing, let him deal with them. We need to get you feeling better again, all this stress is doing you no good!"

Lena got up from the bed and left Fran quietly sobbing herself to sleep.

Back in the living room, Lena sat down on the sofa, closing her eyes, she thought back to the time before her dad's murder. It had only been a matter of weeks, yet it felt longer. The effect on her brothers worried her, she did not know how to help them. Every day she watched her mum become frailer, she was not eating properly and had lost weight, her mobility was extremely poor now as well. Throwing herself back into the sofa cushions, everything around Lena seemed bleak, she was struggling to see the light at the end of the tunnel.

Later that evening Jack appeared with some food shopping.

"Hey, what do you fancy for eating then? I've got all the things on the list you gave me yesterday. There's even a few treats in there for you all!" Placing the carrier bags on top of the kitchen worktop, he turned to look at Lena. He could tell straight away she had been crying, her eyes were all red. "What's going on here then?" He asked, as he stood in front of her. "Don't be telling me some cock and bull story either, you know you can always talk to me love," pulling her into his embrace, she accepted his hug. Time seemed to stand still when she was with him, he always made her feel better.

"Mum has had a bad day! She's in bed sleeping, she cried herself to sleep. The two boys won't come out of their room, I've tried!" Lena could not stop the tears from falling.

"Listen, you have me here to help, let me! You don't need to do this on your own Lena, I'm going to sort this somehow, I'll make it easier for you!" Even as the words left his mouth, Jack did not know where to start, in order to make life easier for his daughter. He just knew he had no choice.

Eventually, both boys came into the kitchen when they smelt the spaghetti bolognaise Jack had cooked up for them all. "I knew the smell would get you in here," he joked, whilst plating up the food for them.

"Lena, go in and see if your Mum is awake, will you please? If she is, ask her if she wants some good grub, eh?"

The boys took a plate each and went into the living room, to eat in front of the tv.

Jack felt under pressure himself. Every time he called in here, he noticed the amount of stress they were all under, yet how they were feeling was out with his control, there was nothing he could do to fix things for them, he could only be present and show his support by doing menial tasks like shopping etc. At least it was a few less things for Lena to concern herself with, she was his main focus. His business was suffering due to his lack of enthusiasm for it, but he still had Daz working on collections and trying to gather information regarding what had happened to Tony. Homelife was a constant war of words with Sylvie. They were living together but not as one. His gut instinct was screaming at him not to trust the woman he had once loved with all of his heart. There was so much going on within his own life outside these four walls, nonetheless, he had found his daughter, and she was his top priority!

Mum said she'll take a wee plate of dinner," said Lena, as she sidled up beside him in the kitchen. Pointing towards the boys, Jack tried reassuring her once more, "See, things are going to be okay," smiling, he grabbed a plate and handed it to Lena, he then plated one up for himself. "Come on, let's join them, then we can have a look at what's still to be done, right!" Lena nodded her agreement at his words, feeling better for having him, in that moment she did not feel so alone anymore!

CHAPTER THIRTY

Leaving Fran's house, Jack decided to pop into The Horse & Cart pub for a quick drink. He was also on the lookout for Kathy Semple and her friend. When Daz left their company the previous night, he had a niggling feeling that they knew or had some involvement in Tony's demise. First thing this morning, he called around to see Jack at his house, explaining what had happened with the two women.

"Boss, I'm telling you, they know something about Tony's attack! They let on they had not heard what happened to him, but there's something shady going on with them...I'm certain of it!" Daz stated, at the same time the kettle boiled.

 "Coffee anyone?" Sylvie offered, trying to inject herself into the conversation. When Daz had appeared so early in the morning, it unnerved her, he never called round in person unless he had important information to share with Jack.

Both men stopped what they were doing to look at her, "Sylv, we're trying to have a conversation here, we don't need you hanging about!" Jack replied. Sylvie stood staring at him across the kitchen before stating, "I was only offering you a bloody coffee, next time I won't bother! All the thanks I get!" She then stormed out of the kitchen, making her way into the next room, where she could still hear what was being said.

"So, you think two bimbos had Tony done over? Seriously?" Jack laughed, "Boss I never said they done him in, but I do seriously believe they have knowledge as to who or why, maybe even both! It's definitely worth having a conversation with them...Just watch that they don't eat you alive, they're a right pair of whollopers!" With that said

Daz got up from the breakfast bar stool, "I'll go see if I can learn anything new today."

Jack finished his coffee, "Yeah, you keep your ears to the ground, I'll catch up with those two, I'll make a point of it!"

Christ Almighty! If he finds out about me, I'm done for!

Sylvie recognised the severity of her actions and the repercussions for all involved, yet it did not stop her from wanting her revenge! Sensing that she could be in deep danger, she decided to get dressed, head into town and start arranging her escape route out of this trouble she had gotten herself into!

Before Jack had the chance to speak to her, she ran upstairs to her dressing room...She needed to stay clear of him as much as she could!

Now standing in the pub, Jack looked all around him, giving the place a once over, mainly for his safety. He was impressed with the decor and there was a good atmosphere within the place. There were a few faces he recognised, but he knew they did not pose any kind of a threat to him, so he relaxed and ordered himself a pint of Guinness with a whisky chaser, after the day he had, he felt he deserved it.

It was getting late, thinking he was not going to catch Kathy or her friend, he decided to have another whiskey before calling it a night, he called over to where the barmaid stood, "Another whiskey doll!" As she placed the glass in front of him, he heard cackling coming from the direction of the entrance, sure as fate, in walked Kathy, arm in arm with a well-dressed man.

The moment she set eyes on Jack standing at the bar, *Shit*! She realised right away this was not a coincidence, he was there for her.
Trying to pretend she had not seen him; Kathy directed her date to the bar then proceeded to order some drinks from the barmaid. Jack had wasted enough of his time waiting about, casually, he approached the pair at the bar. Kathy had watched him walking over, nervously she spoke, "Hi Jack, long time no see!" Dismissing her attempt at being sociable, Jack replied," Yeah, long time Kathy, I think you know why I'm here. Do you want to grab a seat so that we can have a chat?" The man Kathy was with recognised Jack, he was well aware of his reputation, he had no intentions of stepping in, which Kathy soon became aware of as she saw him take a drink from his pint.
Grabbing her handbag from the bar, she followed as Jack led the way over to a table in the corner.

"Right Kathy let's not beat about the bush...I think you know why I'm here, so let's not waste anymore of our time. You tell me what you know about the attack on Tony, and you get to shimmy back to your fella..." He deliberately left his sentence unfinished, allowing her to imagine what she could expect, if she never told him.

Given the change in her demeanour, he felt she had picked up on this herself.

Kathy sang like a canary, telling him everything she knew from accidentally telling Tony who Lenas' real father was, to what she had told the two guys who had virtually broken her door down.

Jack was not surprised to hear what she told him, however, there were parts of her story which did not add up in his mind.

"So, what did Tony say when you told him about me and Fran getting together?"

"Well…He was shocked and angry, calling you all the motherfucks under the sun!" Now that she had told him what had happened, her anxiety levels dropped slightly. "He left Fran and was staying with my pal Maria and her kids," she continued.

"Yeah, he left Fran battered and bruised, she can hardly feckin walk due to him! Bet he didn't tell your mate that…Did he?"

Shocked, she replied, "No, he never uttered a bloody word about that! Is Fran going to be okay? Christ, I feel responsible for all this, if I hadn't let it slip, none of this would have happened!"

"I think there's more to it than that, but it hasn't helped Fran that's for sure!" He replied, before getting up from his seat and walking away, leaving Kathy lost in her thoughts.

CHAPTER THIRTY-ONE

The following morning Jack woke with a thumping sore head, he knew it was due to his lack of sleep, as he had tossed and turned all night. When he arrived home the previous night after talking with Kathy, his mind was racing with different scenarios, trying to work out what the hell was going on. He kept coming back to the same questions; Who had Tony told that he was not Lena's real dad? Why would this news cause him to be murdered? And...Were the guys who had pushed their way into Kathy's place anything to do with his death or meddling in his business dealings? All of these questions whirled around his head most of the night. The one thing, he was certain of, was the fact that he would get to the bottom of it!

Pulling his dressing gown from the chair next to his bed, he put it on and made his way downstairs to the kitchen. "Sylvie!" He called out but there came no reply. Wondering where she was, he made himself a coffee and sat at the breakfast bar, waiting for her. Ten minutes passed, still there was no sign of Sylvie; **Where the bloody hell is she?** It was out of character for her to leave, without her telling him where she was going. Casually, he got up from his seat, then proceeded up the stairs, to look in the bedroom she had last used. With their relationship under pressure and constant quarrelling, Sylvie had taken to sleeping in one of the spare rooms. It suited them both, as they tried to navigate their way through their differences.

"Sylvie, are you in here?" Jack asked, opening the bedroom door. No reply, he entered, surprise hit him, when he realised the bed had not been slept in. **What the hell is she up to?** Startled, he called out her name, as he opened the doors of the other spare rooms, hoping she was in one of them, alas she was nowhere to be found. Eventually, he went into his office and called Daz. He answered on the third ring, "Daz, do you have any idea where my Sylvie is?" When Daz replied that he did not, and that the last time he saw her was the day before at their house, it dawned on Jack, perhaps she did not come home. "Can you remember if she said where she was headed yesterday? Times like now, he wished he paid more attention to her, when she spoke. "No, sorry Boss, she did leave in a hurry though, but I've no idea!" Panic was beginning to set in with Jack, this was the last thing he needed, after what happened to his brother, he was hoping Sylvie had come to no harm. "Get here as soon as you can...I think we might have a problem!"

Daz appeared at the door within the hour. "So, what are you thinking Boss?" He could see the anxiety in Jack, as he was pacing the floor of the sitting room. "I'm not sure but I don't like this one little bit! After what happened to Tony, I don't know...Could it be to do with the botched deal? I'm beginning to think it is, that means it's going to get a whole lot messier!" Jack looked over to where Daz was sitting, "But, you settled most of the money with them, they wouldn't come after you now, they want all of their cash repaid and they were happy with your agreement... They know you're good to your word!" Jack stopped pacing back and forth, "You've got a point there! Anything happens to me or mine, they know it would affect them being paid. So, what the hell is going on then? If it isn't them, then where is she?" Daz was sitting shaking his head from side to side, "Dunno Boss, it's a strange one, but I'm sure we will get her!"

Nodding in agreement, "Yeah, one way or another, we will find out exactly what's going on!"

Instructing Daz to get out and about onto the streets of Glasgow, Jack got himself dressed quickly before he too headed into the city in search of Sylvie, he would begin by visiting some of her friends.

Driving around from door to door, hours passed by, and yet Jack was no further forward, as to Sylvie's whereabouts. All of her friends had no idea where she could be, most saying they had not seen her in months. Jack found this strange, as Sylvie had told him she had been meeting with them in recent weeks.

So...If she hasn't been with her friends, then who the hell has she been meeting with?

Suddenly, it hit him...
The one thing which he knew for certain, the only person he knew she had been seeing was Tony, in Lauders pub. There were CCTV images to prove this, it fitted within the timescale when she was supposed to be meeting with her friends. Jack was struggling to understand why it would take several meetings for Tony to tell her about Lena. It didn't make sense...Unless they had been involved in more dangerous matters...This would explain why he's dead and she's vanished!

CHAPTER THIRTY-TWO

In the days following Tony's funeral the house felt sombre. Fran and Lena both felt a slight sense of relief that it was over. Brian and Ian had attended the funeral, much to Lena's dismay, she felt it would be too much on them, given their behaviour since his death. Nonetheless, they each managed to get through the service, with the emotional support from herself and their mum. Once they had all returned home, the boys broke down in tears, overwhelmed with the day's events. Jack had returned home with them, he reassured Lena that their crying was a good thing, which should help them in coming to terms with their loss.

Fran had overheard this conversation and admitted to Lena that for once, Jack was right. They all agreed to take things a day at a time!

Every morning Fran got herself up and ready, before giving the boys a shout to get up for their breakfast before school. Determined to get back into her physio routine, she had not been practising her exercises, therefore her mobility had lessened, and her pain levels had risen. The recent stress and not pacing herself meant tensions had developed within her back. She understood now, what she had to do, to try and get it into a more manageable situation, thus allowing her a better quality of life for herself and her kids.

Once the kids were out of the door, Fran stood, supported by the sink, whilst she washed the breakfast bowls. Doing small bits of everyday housework tasks meant a lot for her nowadays. It took it out of her physically, yet it also enabled her to feel some kind of normalcy. It was a catch twenty-two scenario, which she played every minute of every day.

No one, but her nearest and dearest, understood that in order for her to do, go or participate in anything, she would pay the high price of a pain flare up, which very often would last for days. So, for Fran, if she went somewhere or tried doing anything, it had to be meaningful, because she was going to suffer, one way or another!

Lost in thought, as she washed the soapy bubbles from her hands, she heard a knocking at the front door. **_Who the bleeding hells this now?_** She was not in the mood for visitors. Drying her hands with the tea towel, she slowly walked to the door, with the aid of her walking stick. Upon answering it, she was shocked at who was standing on her doorstep.

"Hello Fran..."
Speechless, Fran could not prevent herself as she stared at Kathy Semple.

"It's been a long time! I just had to come and see you when I heard what happened to your Tony..." Kathy said nervously.

Suddenly Fran regained her composure, "Kathy...It's been years! You and I both know he was never really just mine! Do you want to come in..." Fran asked, opening the door further to allow Kathy access.

Kathy accepted her offer and crossed the threshold into Fran's house, she followed behind her friend, watching her, as she used her walking stick for support walking up the dimly lit hallway.

Entering the living room, Kathy looked around at the badly decorated room with the worn sofa and chair. It lacked lustre yet she felt comfortable within the space. "Take a seat! Do you want tea or coffee?" Fran was aware of Kathy taking in her surroundings, as she sat in the chair across from the settee, "I'll have whatever you're having," replied Kathy.

Once Fran had made the coffees, she returned to the living room and made herself comfortable on the settee.

"So, you heard about Tony then?" Fran asked. Kathy placed her coffee mug on the table next to her, "Yes! I was actually at the service, but I did not want to make a scene by approaching you there, it wasn't the time or the place! You all done him proud! It was a lovely service." Nervously, she played with her rings on her fingers.

Kathy was unsure whether to tell Fran, about her divulging her secret to Tony before he died. Looking at her old friend now, she felt a tremendous amount of guilt, she could see the difficulties Fran was having with her health. Inside Kathy felt like getting up and running from the room, the remorse eating away at her.

"Thanks, that's kind of you to say. It was mostly Lena and Jack that had to do with the organising. You remember Jack...Don't you!" It was said as a statement, rather than a question, Fran had not forgotten what Tony had told her before he beat the living day out of her. From Kathy's reaction, Fran knew she had struck a nerve with her. Sitting more upright in her seat, Kathy straightened her back, "Of course I remember Jack Davis, everyone knows that name! He's a handsome fella, I'm not going to forget a looker either!" She laughed anxiously, "That's good he helped with his brother's funeral, if I mind right, they weren't too close."
Shifting herself, so that she could place a cushion behind her back for better support, Fran heard the menace in Kathy's reply, she was in no mood for games. "Why don't you come straight out and say why you're really here Kathy! We both know you spoke to Tony, and I'm sat like this because of what you told him!" Rage began coursing through Fran's veins, she was struggling to control herself, if she was more able, she would've frog marched her right out the door. "Fran, if I'd known for one minute you hadn't

told him about Lena's real dad, I swear..." Fran cut her off straight away, "It was never your place to mention Lena or who her father is to anyone! Yet you have the gall to come to my home and what Kathy? What exactly are you here for? I'm not going to accept an apology from you, it's your bloody fault I'm like this!" Fran grabbed the walking stick from her side and banged it on the floor.

Rising from where she sat, Kathy took one step towards the settee, "STOP RIGHT THERE! Don't think of coming near me, if I was more capable believe me you would be on the floor right now! You and your big mouth have caused me and my family no end of troubles. NOW GO! JUST GO!" Fran was screaming, "Calm down, you're going to do yourself more harm!" There was no way Fran was going to be pacified, "CALM DOWN! You have no idea of what you have caused! If you didn't tell Tony, I would still be able to live my life without being in constant bloody pain!" Understanding that she would never be friends with Fran again, "I came here to see how you and your kids were getting on. Yes, I told Tony, and I regret it ever since Jack told me what he had done to you! You canny think I meant for you to end up like this! I hated him for laying a hand on you...That's partly why I told those two big guys that came looking for him, where he was!"

Screwing her eyes up, "What big guys are you talking about?" Fran asked, inhaling a deep breath to try and calm herself. "Ask Jack, I've told him everything I know! I'm sorry for the way things have worked out for you Fran, I really am!" And with that, Kathy picked her handbag off the floor and left the room. Leaving behind Fran with more questions than answers!

CHAPTER THIRTY-THREE

The smell of petrol was overwhelming, her whole body ached from being sat in the same position for hours. If only she could somehow remove the rag which they had used as a blindfold, Sylvie would have a better grasp on her whereabouts, but she couldn't, as her hands were tied behind her.

When she had arranged to meet with Danny O'Brien yesterday, this was the last place she had envisaged herself being! Although, sitting contemplating how she had gotten herself into this situation, she guessed she shouldn't really be surprised.

Months previously, when she had first reached out to him, she understood how dangerous he was. If he did not have the reputation he had, she would never have approached him in the first place for help. At that time, she was bitter and enraged, seeking revenge! Now, as she sat in this dark, smelly place she felt used and humiliated, not to mention gullible, at believing Danny O'Brien's words.

Her first reaction, when Tony had informed her that Jack was indeed Lena's father, was disbelief. ***There is no way! Jack would never lie to me or be able to keep something like this to himself!***
These had been her words, which she had thrown back at Tony. However, once she had digested all of the information, he had given her, then later meeting Lena in person, she knew deep within her heart that Tony was undeniably speaking the truth! It was then she concocted her plan for revenge. She would hit him where it would hurt him the most...his business! It would have the most impact on him and she had enough knowledge of his business dealings to destroy him, the way this news had destroyed her!

In the evenings when Jack was out on business Sylvie stayed at home, crying. During those days, she had to go about her daily business as if nothing had happened. Whilst all the time inside she was awash with a mixture of emotions. One minute she was raging at all the lies he had told her, the next minute she could weep, at the thought of never having her own child, yet knowing he had one with another woman, was the hardest pill to swallow.

The idea came to her one evening, as she sat wallowing in self-pity, drinking a large white wine. Jack was out meeting some big drug dealer from Liverpool, he was wining and dining him in The Corinthian in the town. All that day, he had been on edge, nervous due to the amount of money he was investing in the deal. Thinking about him and the money, it came to her all of a sudden...This was how she would get back at him for treating her like a fool!
Hell Hath No Fury Like a Woman Scorned! You're going to find this out you son of a bitch!
Sylvie thought to herself as she finished off her glass of wine.

Over the coming days and weeks, she watched and listened more intently than she had done previously when Jack discussed his business plans with Daz. It would only be a matter of time until she put her idea into action. When she felt she had enough details on his dealings, she quickly contacted Danny O'Brien. He was a well-known drug dealer who mixed in the same circles as Jack. It was common knowledge that he was just as dangerous as Jack, both men's reputations spoke for themselves. The difference was that Danny O'Brien's business dealings were mostly outside the city. He made his money dealing in county lines, reaching further afield into smaller towns and villages. She knew Jack despised the man, this made what she was about to do even more thrilling for herself.

On their first meeting, she had driven into Edinburgh, as she did not want anyone to notice them. At first glance she felt intimidated by Danny's stature and the intensity of his stare. He had wondered why she was going to all this bother, but once she explained what had happened, he laughed, stating she was one dangerous lady! It had only taken her half an hour to disclose all of Jack's business plans with the Liverpudlians, for Danny to agree that he needed to be taught a lesson, as this deal would also enable Jack to grow out with his area, falling into Danny's territory!

Walking away from their first meeting together, Sylvie had smirked to herself at just how quick and easy it was to bring Jack down. Now, sitting aching all over, she feared for her life as it hit her, at how quickly she had become the target of her own downfall!

CHAPTER THIRTY-FOUR

"Right Daz, what have you got for me?" It had been more than twenty-four hours since Jack had become aware of Sylvie's vanishing act. So far, he had scoured the city centre and all of her friends with no further insight as to her whereabouts. Inside he was panicking, on the outside he was trying his best to try and hide his feelings.
"Boss, I have nothing new! I've been to all of her usual haunts; no-one seems to know where she might be. I am running out of ideas here!" Jack could hear the exasperation on the other end of the telephone line, "Daz, meet me back at mine. We can bang our heads together over a drink, god knows I need one!"

Later, the two men sat in the plush lounge area in Jack's house, nursing their drinks, throwing ideas about, hoping they might come up with a new one. After a few hours of debating whether they were onto something or not with their suggestions, Daz suddenly asked, "So, do you actually know where she was going. If she wasn't meeting her friends?" Jack shook his head in denial, "No...No bloody idea! It's been going around in my head, but I can't seem to come up with anyone, it's niggling me though..." Daz reached over to place his empty tumbler on the glass table in front of him, "Let's look at everything again, we've missed something!"

"Starting from when Tony found out about you being Lena's biological dad, what happened next?"
"Well, as far as we know, that was when he reached out and met with Sylvie to tell her the good news!" Jack replied, sarcastically.
Nodding his head in agreement, Daz continued, "Yeah, then what? Things started going tits up from there for you, didn't they? I mean the coke deal..."
Jack leapt out of his seat, "You think she had something to do with that...Like seriously, I don't think she would go that far, how would she know who to talk to?" Pacing back and forth, Jack continued, "I haven't heard a peep back from our guys on the streets with any names about that feck up! Makes me think it could be someone outside our area..." Jack stopped dead in his tracks, "That fecker O'Brien! He's always had it in for me, the guy hates me almost as much as I hate him! I heard he was striding about the town. Think we should have a wee word with him..."
Sitting shaking his head in disagreement, "Nah,

Boss I don't think she would have the balls to reach out to him, he's a nasty fecker! She wouldn't know how to get in touch with him!" "Ohhh, she's got the nerve all right! She would go out of her way to find him if it meant destroying me, especially after finding out about Lena. I think we need to find O'Brien and find out exactly what's been going on!"

It was late in the evening but still light, as Jack drove his car in the direction of the motorway, heading east, on the hunt for Danny O'Brien. Both men felt trepidation at heading onto his territory. It was common knowledge that O'Brien did not play nice, inside and outside of business. He had a notoriety, which put fear into the hearts of many locals on the East side, just as Jack's did on the West side of the city.
As soon as they crossed into O'Brien's territory, "Well...No going back now!" Stated Daz, watching every corner they drove past, on the lookout for any kind of untoward attention.

"Do you have any idea which pub he uses the most?" Jack asked. "Nope, but I think you'll find whichever one you enter, word will find its way back to him ASAP!" Daz replied. Turning onto the main street, "Right, let's start here, shall we?" Jack turned off the ignition, parking outside a pub called, The Phoenix. Approaching the door into the pub, both men's hearts were racing with anticipation, at what they might come across once inside. They were outside of their comfort zone, if things were to go awry, they would not have the same back up, as they would have on their side of the city. Straightening their backs, they pushed their shoulders back trying to look confident, before entering, "Here goes..." Jack whispered to Daz, upon opening the door to the bar.

The moment they entered, the noise they heard of people chatting and laughing before entering, stopped straight away. Every head in the place turned and stared at the newcomers. "Don't let us interrupt you all!" Jack called out, trying to sound confident. Daz walked up to the bar and ordered two pints of Guinness. Jack followed behind him, all the while surveying the people in the bar, in case he recognised anyone. Once at the bar he stood next to Daz, "Can honestly say I've had warmer welcomes," said Daz, laughing nervously. "I know you can feel it, can't you? The animosity... it's not as friendly here as it is in our locals." Jack nodded at the barman, before taking a drink of his pint.

It was clear they were not going to find out any fresh information from any of the people in the bar, no one had spoken since they had entered. Finishing their drinks, Daz thanked the barman before making their way outside. "Well, that was a friendly place. Thank feck we are out of there, that was awkward, I've never experienced that in my life," Daz began laughing, as they walked towards Jack's car. Just as Jack bent to open the car door, they both looked up to see two black sedans screeching to a halt, a few feet in front of them. "I think Mr O'Brien has come to see us!" Jack stated, as one of the car doors opened and out came Danny O'Brien, flanked by two big burly bodyguards.

"Heard you might be looking for me!" Danny O'Brien called over towards them. "Yeah, you heard right! We don't want to be causing any trouble, we just want to talk..." Jack replied, keeping his eyes on the cars and guys in front of him. "Follow us!" Called O'Brien, getting back inside the car he had come from. Jack and Daz checked with each other, got inside Jack's car then followed on, as the cars sped through the streets. "Stay close, wherever he takes us, we need to stick together. I don't trust this fecker one iota Daz, keep your wits about you!" Jack instructed Daz, his heart and mind racing. The one thing he disliked the most was not being in control, at this moment in time, he had no idea where he was headed or to what he would find!

CHAPTER THIRTY-FIVE

Standing at the kitchen sink washing up the dinner plates and pots, Lena was away in a world of her own, pondering the past few days. "Mum...Have you seen Jack? I'm just thinking I haven't heard from him in a couple of days!" It was unlike him not to be in touch, he had been a constant support for them, especially Lena. "Funny you should ask, no I have not, but I canny wait until I do!" Fran called through from the living room. Ever since her visit from Kathy Semple, Fran's mind had been speculating what she had meant, by insinuating Jack's involvement in Tony's demise. Lying comfortably on the settee, she told herself, he will soon show up. "Cuppa Mum?" Lena called from the kitchen, "Yeah go on then! Are there any kitkats left or have your brothers eaten them all? I could go a wee bit of chocolate," laughed Fran, just as Lena brought her a cup of tea alongside her chocolate biscuit. "There, are you happy now?" Lena jokingly asked. In recent weeks she had noticed the improvement in her mum's mobility and mood. The commitment she was showing towards managing her pain was a massive turnaround from times past, this delighted them all.

The effort her mum was making had not gone unnoticed by the social worker either. The previous week she had made an unannounced visit to them and was amazed at the positive changes within Fran and the household. There would still be good and bad days, but if her mum tried her best to stay positive, the bad days would be nothing like they had been at the start of her pain journey. Encouraged by what she had witnessed on her visit the social worker was putting forward a removal from child protection for them. Fran and Lena were ecstatic at this news, as it meant no more social work involvement. To them both, it felt like the closure of an old chapter in their lives.

"Did you tell the boys about the social worker yet?" Asked Lena, lifting the tv remote from the table, she lay across the chair opposite her mum.

"I did, they were happy, but they don't understand what it really means, they're still too young. I'm over the moon! Feel as though we have passed a test," Fran laughed, looking across at her daughter, she felt immense pride in them both.

"Things are starting to look up for us mum, thank goodness!" It was true, Lena thought to herself. For once, she could relax a bit, go out with the few friends she had kept in touch with from school. Since leaving school, she had been busy looking after her mum and brothers, after the death of Tony. Now, she could think about her future, what she fancied doing as a career. Jack was wanting her to go to college, further her education, he felt she had missed out on so much, due to caring for her mum in the past. Lena declined his offer of financial support to enable her to do so, she preferred to make her own money.

Suddenly, there was loud knocking coming from the front door.

"Who the bleedin hell is that?" Asked Fran, moving into a seated position on the settee. "Stay there mum, I'll go check," Lena replied, walking in the direction of the loud banging. Upon opening the door Lena was no further clear on who was standing on their step. "Is your mum in hen? I need to see her, I've something she needs to know!"
"Who are you?" Lena enquired, "Tell her it's Kathy...Kathy Semple! I'm not here for trouble but I need to tell her something..." Lena heard the urgency in the woman's words, "Hold on. I'll go ask my mum," Closing the front door politely on the woman. "Mum, it's someone called Kathy Semple, says she has something to tell you. It seems important, will I tell her to come in?"
Fran turned to face Lena standing at the living room door, "Aye, I suppose so. Tell her to come in then."
"Fran, I'm not wanting to fight with you! I just heard something in the pub that you would want to know!" Proclaimed Kathy, whilst walking into

the living room. "Aye, what's that?" Fran replied, nonchalantly. Kathy sat next to Fran on the settee, "Well, I was in McVees, in the town, when I heard three guys have a conversation about Jack's missus. It's Sylvie, right?" Fran gave her a side glance, "Aye, but I'm honestly not interested in her. I couldn't tell you anything about the woman!" Exasperated, "Well...You might be once I tell you what I overheard!" Kathy replied. "They were laughing, because they heard that Jack Davis's missus had gone elsewhere to have a problem sorted! The jokes on Jack, they were saying he wasn't up to the job himself, so got her to ask!" Confusion written all over her face, "What the hell you on about Kathy? You're not making one ounce of sense! I'm sure Jack is more than capable of sorting out his own problems. He doesn't need help from anyone else!"

"Fran! You're not getting what I'm telling you! It was your Tony! They said she got someone from the East side to do your man!"

Shocked, Fran asked," Who? Who killed Tony?" Glad to have her attention now, Kathy continued, "Well, from what they were saying it was Danny O'Brien. I don't know if you've heard of him, but he's a big name on the other side of the town. Into similar things to Jack. But, if you think about it, the person who killed your Tony, is the Sylvie one...She's the one that made the request, apparently!"

Fran and Lena sat dumbfounded at the words coming from Kathy's mouth. The thought of Sylvie arranging to have Tony killed would never have entered any of their heads, until now! They were not even aware of them knowing one another.

"NO! It's rubbish!" cried Lena. The thought of Sylvie going out of her way to get to her mum like this, made no sense whatsoever! The only reason Sylvie could possibly have to harm Tony would be to make her mum suffer. Guilt and anger began coursing through Lena's veins, as it dawned on her...She was the reason Tony was dead!

Hysteria took over, "I'm the reason he is dead! She killed Tony because of me!" Lena was screaming at the top of her lungs. "NO! It is nothing to do with you! They must have come across one another because of something else, you know what he was like...Always playing someone for his own benefit!" Fran was frantically trying to calm her down, to no avail. "It IS my fault! It's because she found out Jack's my real dad! She wants to hurt us both! And she's succeeded!"

Kathy stood up between Fran and Lena. "Listen! We don't know why she did what she did! Lena, your mum's probably right, Tony was up to all sorts, with women from everywhere. He probably did her wrong without knowing who she was! Calm down, this is not helping anyone at the moment!" Moving towards Lena, Kathy gently placed her hands on her shoulders, "What you say I make us a cuppa, maybe help calm us all down, then we can decide where we go from here!"

CHAPTER THIRTY-SIX

Up ahead, the cars they had followed stopped outside what looked like an old oil distillery. Jack pulled on the brake and stopped the engine, "Whatever you do, keep your guard up, don't let it slip for one minute! Those are nasty feckers!" Daz stared straight ahead, watching as Danny O'Brien got out of the first car, followed on by four other big guys. He turned, gesturing with his head for them to follow on behind. Getting out of the car, Jack felt as though his whole body was hypervigilant. Adrenaline was coursing through him; he knew Daz well enough to know he would be feeling the exact same way. Giving Daz a nod of his head, they both walked in the direction, following behind Danny O'Brien into the old warehouse.

Inside was dark, the air was thick with the strong smell of oil all around, he could feel it in his nostrils. Assessing their surroundings, both himself and Daz seemed to notice at the same time, someone tied to a chair up ahead of them. Daz stopped dead in his tracks, "Boss, I don't like this one bit! There's someone up there...Look!" Pointing straight ahead.

"Ahhh, so you've spotted our little surprise then!" Danny O'Brien called out. "Thought we would make this feel more homely for you Jack! Make sure your missus would be waiting on you just in case you were missing each other!" Jack and Daz looked at each other, "What the feck!" Said Daz, under his breathe. Unsure how he was going to play this one, Jack remained silent, hoping O'Brien would disclose more regards to Sylvie being where she was. He was still unsure as to why he had found her in this position.

Moving next to where Sylvie sat, O'Brien stroked her face, "Such a pretty lady! Would hate to destroy such beauty!" Sylvie pulled her head away from his touch, "Not so fast now beautiful Sylvie! You were the one who came looking for me, remember!" He was toying with her, he watched as fear enveloped her. Turning, he stared at Jack, "You really should keep your woman on a tighter leash Mr Davis. It would appear that you upset this beauty, right here! Why else would she come running to me for help!" Ahead, Jack stared straight back. He could see how much enjoyment his nemesis was getting from this. It was beginning to make sense now, why Sylvie was here in the first place. The fact she had meddled in his business plans, had cost him a fortune in cash. He felt like turning his back and leaving her in the hands of O'Brien.

"You can keep the lying bitch! I don't want her!" Jack called out towards O'Brien, who was still standing next to Sylvie. "Nonsense! You don't really want me to have your woman, just like you didn't want me having all the areas, which are already mine! You thought you would come and interfere in my business...Didn't you? Take what wasn't yours to have!" The menace in his voice was clear for them all to hear, "But, you were not counting on this beauty coming to ask for my help with her problem!" Next to him, Sylvie began squirming in her seat, "Jack! Please...I'm sorry! Please...Help me!" She cried out, hoping he would forgive her, knowing what lay ahead for her, if he did not.

"Give me a minute with her! We have some unfinished business that needs clearing up first!" Jack calmly requested, conscious of not showing any weakness from his side, he walked forward, until he was standing right in front of Sylvie. Terrified of what was going to happen to her, Sylvie continued pleading for Jack to help get her free. "SHUT UP WOMAN!" It was O'Brien, "I'll give you five minutes with her, then I want you to tell me how you're going to make this up to me...After all, your little domestic has caused me a lot of grief!" Walking away from Sylvie, he ordered his men out of the warehouse, "There's nowhere for them to go, it's safe to leave them. C'mon..." He ushered them out, including Daz.

When it was just the two of them left, Sylvie began crying hysterically. In between sobs, she repeated how sorry she was, for getting them into this situation. Jack stood glaring at her, "Shut up! You are pathetic, you know that right? What the bloody hell made you end up here like this?" Sylvie sobbed uncontrollably, "I'm sorry, I didn't mean for any of this to happen, honestly, you have to believe me Jack!" Infuriated, "BELIEVE YOU! You are having a feckin laugh! If you were not so conniving in the first place, both of us wouldn't be here like this! Tell me, why...WHY?" He was losing his patience with her, "Why would you want to destroy my business so badly?" Sylvie spoke between sobs, "I wanted to hurt you, the way you hurt me! For years we have failed at having a baby. It is all I've ever wanted! Meanwhile, you've had a daughter all this time tucked away...Your dirty little secret! How did you think that was going to make me feel...EH?" She spat the words from her mouth.

Shaking his head from side to side, in disbelief, Jack replied, "So, you thought that gave you the right to ruin us? Running to O'Brien? Wasn't the smartest move Sylv! You have no idea who you're dealing with...He's one dangerous motherfucker!" Frantically, Sylvie began wriggling in her seat, pulling at the ties around her hands, "Jack, you need to help free me, he'll kill me, just like he did Tony!" Stunned at this statement, Jack replied, "What do you mean, killed Tony. What does Tony have to do with him?

His head was beginning to hurt, he was struggling to take in what she was telling him. "When I first found out about your wee secret, it was Tony who told me. He was seeking revenge for all the lies Fran had told him throughout the years, he felt like a fool, believing the girl was his. I was much the same, I was hurting Jack. I knew the way to really cause you pain was in your pocket, so I told O'Brien about the coke deal. Then Tony began threatening me, saying he was going to tell you it was me that got your shipment busted. I asked O'Brien to put the frighteners on him to shut him up, I didn't say kill him!" Jack stepped back in astonishment. "This is getting worse by the second. I can't see how I can help you Sylv, you've got yourself deep in the shit here! Seriously, there's no way in hell he's going to allow you to walk out of that door. You know too much!" Tears began falling from her face, "Don't you think I can't see that! If he's going to kill me, then he'll kill you and Daz as well!" She had a point; his life and Daz's was in danger now all because of her. With one quick move, he pulled his revolver from his waistband and shot her dead!

Upon hearing the shots being fired, O'Brien, his men and Daz ran into the warehouse, to find Jack standing over her limp body. "What the feckin hell have you done?" Daz called out, as he and the other men stood looking stunned. This was the last thing any of them thought would happen, especially O'Brien. He approached Jack, "Well, you've saved me a job, I suppose. I was going to have to teach her a lesson myself! You are one mean fecker Davis!" Jack placed his gun back inside his trouser waistband, then turned to face him, "I think that makes us quits now!" He stated, then without waiting for a reply, he turned and walked out of the warehouse, followed on by Daz, Sylvie's body left hanging lifeless on the chair behind them!

CHAPTER THIRTY- SEVEN

The drive back into the city centre was a quiet one. Both men were startled, at the turn of events the night had taken. Jack had surprised himself with his own actions!

It was not until he had parked up the car, that he spoke, "Daz, I'm as shocked as you are at the way things have turned out tonight! I knew straight away, I had to take her out. I had no choice, after what she told me, it was either her or us, or both if O'Brien had his way!" He could see the shock still on Daz's face and heard the disbelief as he spoke, "Boss, never for a minute would I have believed you capable of killing her! I mean that was your Sylvie back there! Whatever she told you must be bad, in order for you to have done that!"

With Daz's words ringing in his ears, he began running his hands through his hair, the enormity of what he had done was causing his breathing to fasten, he felt as though he couldn't catch a breath properly. "Calm down Boss! You're gonna end up having a heart attack! Concentrate on slowing your breathing down, looks like you're having a panic attack! Slow..." Daz watched his Boss gasping for air, whilst he was trying to calm him down.
Eventually, Jack's breathing slowed, and he regained some composure.
"Do you feel up to telling me what went on in that warehouse between you two? Daz asked.

"It all started with Tony finding out about Lena!" Jack replied.
"I thought that was going to cause trouble when you first told me. I couldn't see Sylvie taking that one lying down, to be honest!"
"That's not the worst of it! After Tony told her, they concocted a plan to get me back. She had overheard our conversations about the business deals we had planned. Thought it would be a good idea to go running to O'Brien, to tell him.

Only, she wasn't thinking of who she had discussed this wee plan with...Tony, he had other ideas. When the deal got blown apart, he decided he was going to make some extra cash, so he began blackmailing her. Told her, he was going to spill the beans to me." Daz was amazed at what he was hearing, "Feck's sake!" Nodding his head, Jack continued, "So, she couldn't have that happen, so she goes running back to O'Brien, asks him to put the frighteners on Tony, to shut him up. Only, she wasn't planning on them shutting him up for good! With all the Police activity around due to Tony's murder, O'Brien had no choice but to get Sylv and make sure she never spoke either! You see, once he knew she had told me, he would have done us both in as well. She left me no choice, it was kill her or be killed!"

Daz sat open-mouthed, processing what he had just been told.
"I know it's a lot to take in, but if I hadn't shot her, we would be lying dead somewhere right now!" Jack was trying to reassure Daz that he had done the right thing, although he still wasn't sure deep down within himself. Finally, Daz spoke, "I know...For what it's worth I think you did the right thing! I think we need to come up with a story to cover her disappearance now, people are going to be asking where she is!"
"I'll say she's left me. Well, she has, in a manner of speaking." He gave a small chuckle. "Yeah, but you'll need to be a bit more specific Boss! Folk are going to want some details..."

"I'm sure once word gets out about me having a secret daughter, that'll be enough reason for Sylv to have done one!"

Agreeing with his reasoning, Daz asked, "What about O'Brien? Can he be trusted to keep his mouth shut about everything?"

"He won't say a word! If he talks, he could be earning himself a hefty jail term. He killed Tony after all, plus he has her body to dispose of, so I don't think he'll be shouting from any rooftops, do you?"

Feeling slightly reassured, Daz relaxed into his seat. Then he had another thought, "What about Fran and Lena, are you telling them what's happened? I mean it involves them, in a way, at least they should know who killed Tony!"

The same thought had already crossed Jack's mind. "Right at this very minute. I'm saying we don't say a word! Let's sleep on it!"

With that, he put the key in the ignition, the car came to life, as they drove away, heading to drop Daz off home.

Upon entering his own house, Jack finally allowed himself to relax. He threw his car keys on top of the sideboard in the hallway, before going into his office, where he poured himself a large whiskey. Sitting in his office, within his quiet, empty home, he felt the adrenaline leave his body. As it did, Jack Davis, Glasgow hard man, sat and wept uncontrollably, at the loss of his Sylvie, the woman he had loved!

CHAPTER THIRTY-EIGHT

Early the next morning, he woke up to the sound of the doorbell. Checking the time on his watch on the bedside table, he noticed it was only nine thirty. Gradually, he got out of his bed, then proceeded down the stairs, to find out who was making all the noise.

When he opened the door, he was taken back to find Lena standing on his doorstep. Relieved to have finally found him, "Oh, you are alive then! We have been worried about you, since you haven't been in touch, we usually hear from you at least once a day!" Exasperated, Jack just shrugged his shoulders, before replying, "Hello to you too! I've just had a lot on with some business dealings. Nothing to worry your pretty little head about!" Yawning, he stood back from the door, allowing her to come in.

Walking into the kitchen, Lena followed behind him. "Have you eaten breakfast yet?" He asked her. "No, I got up and came straight here!" She replied, pulling a seat out from beneath the breakfast bar. Opening the fridge door, Jack said, "Do you fancy some scrambled eggs? I could pop in some toast, if you want?" Lena's stomach rumbled; she had not eaten since early the previous day. Fran and her were both too concerned about Jack to have been worried about eating, Hence the reason she had left the house first thing, in order to put their minds at ease.

Looking around, she took in the gorgeous, luxurious surroundings. Even the kitchen was stunning in this house. It had beautiful cream marble worktops, which contrasted with the darker shade on the floor. They had all mod cons, she loved the big American style fridge freezer, which probably held enough food to feed an army, she thought to herself.

"Is Sylvie still asleep? I hope she's not going to be mad at me, for turning up so early!" She was lying, Lena had taken an instant dislike to the woman the night they had first met. The feelings were mutual, she could see it in her eyes, the way she watched Lena's every move, as though she was going to steal something. "She's not here! She's not going to be coming back either. She's left me!" Hoping this would suffice, yet knowing Lena, he continued, "Apparently, she did not fancy becoming a step-mum!" He laughed at his own joke.

Dismayed by his casual attitude, Lena screwed her eyes up, "That's not funny!" Hearing the hurt in her voice, Jack approached her, placed his arms around her shoulders and gave her a hug, "I'm sorry, I'm not really good at dealing with emotional things. She was angry at me for not telling her all about you! I should have told her, there was a chance you would show up one day!" Lena thought about telling him what Kathy Semple had said to her mum, however, she felt it would be best coming directly from Fran herself. "After breakfast, I think you should come back with me. My mum has some interesting news you will want to hear!"

The hairs on Jack's arms raised at Lena's words, wondering what she could be talking about, he dismissed the idea that she would know about Sylvie's demise. It was too soon.
"Right, let me get freshened up, then we'll head over, does that sound okay?"
Lena nodded in agreement, looking forward to her breakfast being made by someone other than herself, would make it all the more tastier.

Arriving home with Jack in tow, Lena felt quite smug. Another problem she had solved, "Here Mum, look who I found!"
Fran popped her around her bedroom door, "Two wee minutes hen, I'm just getting ready." It had taken all of her strength to drag herself from her bed this morning. Throughout the night, Fran had tossed and turned with the aches in her

back and legs, she could not find a comfortable position. It was no wonder she felt like death warmed up this morning. Hoping for an early night, she had already planned her day, resting as much as she could, a nice warm bubble bath then bed. *I just need to get through the day first!* She told herself, grabbing her walking stick, as she made her way, slowly, towards the living room.

Jack and Lena were sitting next to each other on the settee, when she appeared, Jack got up and moved onto the chair nearest the window. "Have you had a rough night?" He asked Fran, she looked tired, and her movements were slow. He had spent enough time in her company to tell when she was experiencing a bad day. "Yeah, do I look that bad? Took me ages to fall asleep, then when I did, I woke up with the pain, today is not a good pain day!" Lena shuffled up closer to her mum, "Is there anything I can get you Mum? Have you had all your meds?" Nodding, Fran replied, "Yes, I took them a bit earlier than usual. Will you make me a coffee please hen?"
"Sure, you fancy one as well?" Lena asked Jack, as she got up from her seat. "Yeah, why not. Since you are already boiling the kettle," he answered.

With Lena in the kitchen preparing the hot drinks, Fran took the opportunity to tell him what Kathy Semple had said regarding what had happened to Tony. When she had finished relaying the information to him, she was rather annoyed at his lack of concern. "Have I just wasted my breath telling you all that?" Caught off guard by the accusatory tone of her voice, he said, "No, why would you think that?"

"You don't seem shocked, that's why! When we first heard, we were gobsmacked! Or do you know something we don't?" Jack's heart began racing again, his palms sweating, he was not sure how to answer this. He had agreed with Daz that they would not tell anyone what had happened with O'Brien. However, he was feeling the pressure sitting here in front of Fran, he did not like lying to her or Lena, yet he was unsure as to how much they could handle.

Deciding to keep his mouth closed for the foreseeable, he let out a sigh of relief when Lena came in carrying the coffee mugs.

"Your Mum has just told me about Kathy Semple. I will try my best to find out the truth, then we will see what needs to be done. That's okay with you?" Lena lowered her head, "Listen to me Lena, whatever happened to Tony had nothing to do with you...I mean that!"

He hated seeing her so downtrodden, at the end of the day he would need to tell them both the truth. Today was not the day!

CHAPTER THIRTY-NINE

Jack had stayed long enough to finish his coffee before he left to meet with a business partner. Fran was left with an uneasy feeling. There was something not quite right with Jack, she had no idea what it was, but her gut instinct was yelling at her. From the moment he had entered with Lena, he was acting strangely, not his usual confident debonair self. Perhaps, it was due to Sylvie finding out about their affair from years previous. He was being flippant with his replies, as to her questions about how Sylvie had reacted, what she had said etc. He had not answered her clearly, when she had enquired, as to where Sylvie might have gone, or who she had to turn to, for support in dealing with the bombshell. Fran accepted that if the shoe were on the other foot, and she had just discovered that her partner had a secret love child, she would be heartbroken, angry and in need of gentle support and care. Jack seemed unconcerned when she had put this to him, it was as though he had totally detached himself from his feelings for Sylvie.

"Do you think he was okay?" Lena asked. Fran, who had been sitting thinking just the same thing, replied, "I'm not so sure he is you know, I thought he was a bit aloof about the whole Sylvie thing. Maybe just a man thing!" She did not wish for any more worries to be placed upon Lena's young shoulders regarding adult relationships. During the night, she had heard her daughter crying in her bedroom. Fran knew it was due to what Kathy Semple had told them both. Lena was blaming herself for Tony's death. No matter how many times she had tried to explain that it was nothing to do with her, it seemed to fall on deaf ears. Fran watched Lena, as she sat staring out of the window, "You're away in a wee world of your own there! Are you okay? You're worrying about Jack, when you need to focus on yourself. It's the school holidays, why don't you go out, see some friends?" Lena turned to face her mum, "I'm alright, I just think he wasn't telling us the truth. When I was sitting in his kitchen earlier, he was busy making us breakfast. I noticed Sylvie's make up bag sitting along the counter. Now are you telling me, she would go away without her stuff. It's Sylvie we are talking about, she's never without a full face on!"
Fran had to admit she had a point, "Aye, you're right there! Maybe she left in a hurry though. If they had been arguing, she might not have been thinking straight..." Looking at Lena's face, she knew she wasn't taking in her excuses, "Nah Mum, no way would Lady Muck leave without her precious beauty products, she's too into

herself to leave without them! He's hiding something!"

"Well...Whatever it is, will come out eventually. That's the thing about the truth, it doesn't stay hidden for long! Now, will you please go out and stop worrying!"

Fran convinced Lena that she would be fine resting. So, Lena got herself ready to go catch up with her friends from school. It was the one thing which pleased Fran the most, seeing Lena reunite with her friends. Having spent so much of her young life stopping in to care for herself and her brothers, she delighted in watching her getting ready, then listening, as Lena told her all the girlie gossip on her return. Checking the time on the clock on the mantelpiece, she saw it was time for the boys to get up or they would miss their football training. They had both joined one of the local junior football teams. It was doing them both good, mixing with other kids and exercising. The difference in their behaviours was the most noticeable, having struggled with all of the changes recently, they were coming on well.

Later, when she had at last the house to herself, Fran lay on the settee thinking back, especially, over the past year and a half.

At the beginning, when she had been first diagnosed with her condition, she had struggled with the idea of a life with pain. Her life had already been far from happy, due to her love of the drink. It was only as she reminisced, the enormity of what her family had endured hit her! Every day, waking up, unsure if she could move from the bed herself, feeling so fed up, she often had thoughts of not wanting to go on with her life. It was her family that had not only cared for her physical needs but had given her the mental strength to power through her days. So much had changed since those early days.

Nowadays, she was living with pain, she was not allowing the pain to take away her enjoyment for the simple things in life. This included seeing her kids going out and enjoying spending time doing things they loved doing. As long as she micro-managed her time as best she could and paced herself, she knew this was the answer to having more productive days. No-one understood the extent of thought which had to go into everything, from how she moved her body, how far things were to reach or how long she could sit and stand. People could not see how sore her body was, therefore, a lot of them misunderstood that it was always there, just varying degrees. One day Fran hoped to be mobile enough to join them in some of their new activities, but she accepted it was still a day at a time.

The one thing she knew for certain was that she and her family were resilient and with their shared determination they would get through anything!

CHAPTER FORTY

"Thank feck that's done with Boss!" Daz
proclaimed. They were walking away from The
Corinthian in the city centre, having met with
new associates from Turkey. "Couldn't agree
more...We needed that though, it went to plan, I
think!" Ever since he had shot Sylvie, Jack's head
was all over the place, he was second guessing
himself. Picking up on his indecision Daz tried
reassuring him. "Yeah it went well... Once they
send the gear, we can start distributing it and we
are back in business Boss!" Jack nodded his
agreement, crossing the road, heading towards
his parked car, Daz following behind him.

In the distance, someone caught Daz's eye,
"Here, Boss is that not O'Brien up there?"
Pointing across, to the opposite side of the road.
Jack stopped dead in his tracks to see where Daz

was pointing towards. Sure, as anything, strutting along the street in the direction of The Corinthian was Danny O'Brien. "What the feck! Do you think he's headed where we've just left?" Daz heard the frustration in Jack's voice. "Looks like they could be. What are you going to do about it? Surely, the Turks are not thinking of supplying him as well. That's well sneaky Boss!" Turning on his heels, Jack marched across the road, walking until he came face to face with his nemesis once again.

Stopping right in front of Danny O'Brien, Jack blocked his pathway. "Are you going somewhere nice?" Smirking, O'Brien replied, "If you'll get out of my way, I have a very important business meeting to attend Mr Davis!" Jack remained where he was, "There's only one reason you're here and I think you've been given the wrong idea! You see, the deals already completed, you've no need to walk any further here!" O'Brien laughed before replying, "No, I think you are the one who has been given the wrong idea! You see, I was invited along here today by our Turkish friends. It would appear that they feel there is enough good product to go around. So, if you don't mind removing yourself out of my way!" Remaining firmly where he stood, Jack was enraged at O'Brien, raising his voice, "I'm not asking you to leave here right now, I'm telling you! Now... GET YOUR ARSE OFF MY TURF!"

Unperturbed, Danny O'Brien stood his ground. Quietly and calmly stating, "Mr Davis, need I remind you of our last meeting and what became of your once beautiful Sylvie? I don't think for one minute You are in any way in the position to order ME anywhere!" The blood drained from Jack's face, standing beside him Daz was unsure if his Boss should push O'Brien any further. He did not want to end up fighting here on this Glasgow street, nor did he wish to be spending his years locked up in jail for assisting a murder. Nudging Jack, Daz signalled with a nod of his head for him to step out of O'Brien's way.

Seeing that Daz had given Jack a nudge to move, O'Brien chuckled, "Listen to your man Jack, get out of the way, before I have a change of heart and inform the old bill where they can find your Sylvie! One anonymous tip off and you ain't going to be walking these streets for a long time!" Taking the threat at face value, Jack stepped closer to O'Brien's face, "I'm only letting you continue on your way because if you get your deal with them, you're going to stick to your own patch! It's the only way any one of us is going to get along. Don't be thinking threatening me about Sylv is going to work either...You were there! It was on your patch that she disappeared. It seems we both have a lot to lose if old Bill finds out what happened to her!"

Jack sensed that in O'Brien's change in demeanour, he had hit a nerve. Taking a few steps backwards, "You're right, there's plenty of gear to go about, as long as you stick to your turf, I'll stick to mine!" Both men agreed to share the deal, meaning that they had resolved their fears of losing their business, without losing face in front of their men.

With that said, Jack stepped sideways, allowing O'Brien to carry on in the direction of The Corinthian and the Turks.

"Feck, that was a close one Boss!" Exclaimed Daz, as they got into Jack's car. "For a minute there I saw myself behind bars! That was quick thinking the way you changed that around. You think he'll stick to his word?" Sweat was dripping down Jack's spine, he had come to the decision only to save himself and his business. In that moment, it had not dawned on him that Daz may well become collateral damage. Relieved it had worked out to his benefit and Daz's.

"Yeah, Yeah, he has a lot to lose, just like us! There's no way I'd have given him the opportunity if I thought for a minute he'd screw us over! Been through too much to let that arsehole cost us anymore..."

CHAPTER FORTY-ONE

Driving through the city centre streets, Jack was struggling to keep his mind focussed. Sitting next to him, Daz was humming along to a tune on the radio. He recognised the tune but could not remember the name of the song or who was singing it, usually he was an expert on music, frustrated at his lack of knowledge, he shook his head and drove on.

"What's up Boss?" Daz stopped humming along to the radio when he saw Jack shake his head.

"Nothing...I'm just annoyed at myself. I can't remember things which I should be able to, perhaps it's old age creeping in now!" He joked, but Daz could see how troubled he was looking.

"Aye, old age! Or maybe recent events aren't helping you either. Have you been sleeping?" Knowing that he was having problems trying to sleep himself, Daz felt that Jack would be experiencing the same, if not worse emotions, but he also knew him well enough to know he would try his best to hide this, rather than admit it to anyone.

"I'm fine...It's only natural, I'm a bit tired, I have a lot on my mind. I went to see Fran. Lena turned up at my place, asking questions about Sylvie. I hate lying to them! I think I'll need to explain the situation to them!"

Daz turned quickly, staring at Jack, "Boss, I don't think that's one of your better ideas! Surely, if you tell them what you did, they'll grass!"

"I'm almost certain that they won't tell anyone, I think when they discover it was her that set Tony up, they will be glad she's away! Lena is blaming herself for his demise, I canny stand back watching her crucify herself for something she had absolutely nothing to do with!" With that said, Daz raised his eyebrows and nodded in agreement.

Having dropped Daz off back home for the day, Jack continued on his way towards Fran's place. He had decided whilst talking with Daz that the time had come to tell her about Sylvie's involvement in Tony's murder. Inside, he was not as convinced as he made out to Daz about her loyalty towards him. Therefore, he was slightly anxious about telling her the truth. He owed it to her though, more so his Lena, she had suffered enough!

Walking straight into Fran's house, he smiled to himself, hearing the usual commotion between Lena and her brothers. There was very rarely a time when he had entered this house to find tranquillity. Listening as he walked along the hallway towards the living room, brought him back into the present moment and what he was about to disclose. Reassuring himself he could disclose the information, without causing further pandemonium.

"Hey! What's with all the noise? I could hear you all, before I saw you!" Jack stated, entering the living room. Finding both the boys scrambling on the floor with Lena standing at the side, trying her best to create peace. Stopping, Brian looked up, "Uncle Jack, it's him…It's his fault! He won't give me back the tv remote!" Pointing at Ian, who was lying sprawled across the carpet, beneath his brother. "Boys, it's only a tv remote, now c'mon I'm sure we can resolve this in a grown-up manner. What you say, you both get up off the floor." Sheepishly, both boys did as they were asked. Ian gave Brian the remote control, then threw himself onto the settee in a huff. "Thank God you appeared!" Stated Lena exasperated. "I've only been telling those two eejits to quit carrying on for the past twenty minutes! You walk in and look…it's a miracle…" Jack smiled, "Yeah, that's me, a miracle worker! Where's your Mum?" Thinking Fran was still in bed, "She's at the physio this morning but she's due back soon. Are you staying?" Thankful for a bit of time to get his head straight and work out how he was going to break this news to her, Jack agreed to wait until she returned.

He had just finished helping Lena do the housework when Fran returned from the health centre. "BY JEEZUS! There's a sight I thought I'd never see…Jack Davis with a cloth in his hand cleaning up! You're usually the one making the mess!" Fran stood laughing, as she took the sight of Jack and Lena cleaning together.
"HA! HA! HA! Very feckin funny! Just thought I'd make myself useful while I waited on you!" He replied, finishing up dusting the mantelpiece. Fran removed her jacket, then sat on the chair

next to where he stood, "Waiting on me?" She asked suspiciously. "Why? What's happening now?" Shifting herself to get comfortable, she looked up at Jack next to her. "There is something we need to discuss..." Jack's eyes moved from Fran's face to Lena's. "Boys...Do you fancy some sweets from the shop?" Both the boys jumped off the settee towards him, "Here, now share that!" Handing Brian the money, the boys put their trainers on before running down the hall and out of the door.

Hearing the slamming of the front door, Jack could feel the anxiety build within him. Now that he was here with them both in front of him, he was not sure where to begin. ***Here goes***! He told himself.

"Lena, why don't you sit down as well..." Lena drew her eyes upwards, "Oh no! It's something really bad if you're telling me I need a seat!" She exclaimed, moving over she sat on the settee opposite Fran. Jack kept his head down, pacing back and forward, whilst he relayed what had really happened to Tony and the consequences, which resulted in Sylvie's demise!

CHAPTER FORTY-TWO

Fran and Lena sat dumbfounded at what Jack had just told them. Neither one could take in the enormity of the situation at first, "So, Sylvie had Tony done in, then done a runner?" It was Fran who spoke first. Placing his hands on her shoulders, he replied, "Fran, she has not done a runner! Listen to what I've just said..." Moving his hands from her shoulders, she replied, "Don't patronise me, Jack! You've just told us how Sylvie arranged everything and now she won't be coming back!" Dread and fear were coursing through Jack. He did not have the heart to come straight out and explain how HE had shot Sylvie, struggling to find the words, he continued, "Fran...When I found out the lengths she had gone to, there was only one way out for her..." Still, Fran and Lena sat staring up at him with puzzled expressions on their faces. Finally, Lena broke the silence, "Are you saying that she's not coming back 'cause she's dead as well?" Fran let out a gasp, "Is she right Jack, is Sylvie dead?"

There was no other way to get out of this now, Jack had to clarify what he was trying to say to them.

"Sylvie is dead...I shot her!"

Both Fran and Lena caught their breath, the atmosphere in the room went ice cold.
"YOU! YOU KILLED SYLVIE! Are you feckin mad?" Appalled, Fran fell back into the chair, "Seriously Jack! Is that what you are telling us?"

Lena pulled her knees up under herself on the settee, curling herself away from him, he felt terrible, watching his daughter withdraw from him.

"Calm down Fran!" He said, trying to remain calm himself, "It wasn't like you think! When we were left in that warehouse, just the two of us, it became clear to us both O'Brien was not going to let us leave alive. I had to do it! It was kill her or both of us would be killed anyway! She knew too much, plus she had Tony killed...It was all her doing!" As hard as he tried to convince them he had to do it, watching the horror on their faces, told him he was not winning them over.

It seemed like time standing still, as they all processed what had been said. Jack felt emotionally exhausted, moving towards Lena on the settee, he sat down alongside her, aware of her flinching further into it.

"Listen, I never wanted any of this! When I first discovered what Sylv had been up to, I was as flabbergasted as you two... Believe me!" Letting out a long sigh, he continued, "There's no way I would have shot her if I thought for a minute, we were both walking out of that place. O'Brien had us both, plus Daz!" Removing her hands from her face, "Jack, I can't take this in. I'm really struggling to get my head around this, I canny believe YOU shot her. For Christ's sake man you were supposed to be in love with her!" Fran had to restrain herself, she wanted to get up and walk straight out of the room, away from him!

Putting his head down, "I did love her! But Fran, you need to understand the way it was. I had no choice; she had given me no choice! She had Tony killed...She also cost me a lot of money interfering in my business dealings. But...The money wasn't the reason. If I hadn't shot her, I would not be here now! I need you both to believe me...PLEASE!" Aware he was pleading, Jack felt he had nothing else to lose. The last thing he wanted was for these two to turn their backs on him, he needed them!

Fran looked over to where Lena was, "What's your thoughts on all of this? You've been a hell of a quiet!" Lena stared across at her mum, she felt physically sick, but she was not going to admit that she could see how deflated Jack was next to her. When she had first met with Jack again, she had felt an instant connection, even before finding out his true identity. He had become a big part of her life, incredibly supportive towards her and the rest of the family. Her brothers looked up to him, she could see the way her mum looked at him, she could not imagine her life without him in it now!

"I don't understand it all either, but she did get Tony murdered, it was her fault, so for that, I am glad she's dead! I never liked her anyway!" Jack put his hand flat out on the settee, Lena reached over and grabbed it. "I believe you! I'm glad that you are still here!" That was all it took, for the floodgates to open, as tears fell from Jack's face.

When Lena saw the tears falling from Jack's face, she automatically sidled up to him, wrapping her arms around him, she gave him a big hug. Fran watched them from her seat, confused and bewildered at Jack's treatment of Sylvie, yet it did not stop her heart swelling with the love she felt, seeing her daughter comforting her dad.

 "Alright you two...That is enough for one day! You'll have me crying in a minute! It's going to take some time to allow all of this to sink in, but we will get through this...Together!

THE END

Printed in Great Britain
by Amazon

38327410R00106